The
PRINCESS DIARIES

Mia Goes Fourth

Meg Cabot

D0981710

MACMILLAN CHILDREN'S BOOKS

First published 2002 by Macmillan Children's Books
a division of Macmillan Publishers Limited
20 New Wharf Road, London N1 9RR
Basingstoke and Oxford
www.panmacmillan.com

Associated companies throughout the world

ISBN 0 330 41544 1

1 3 5 7 9 8 6 4 2

A CIP catalogue record for this book is available from
the British Library.

Typeset by Intype London Ltd
Printed and bound in Great Britain by
Mackays of Chatham plc, Chatham, Kent

Many thanks to the usual suspects: Beth Ader, Jennifer Brown, Barb Cabot, Sarah Davies, Laura Langlie, Abby McAden, David Walton and especially Benjamin Egwatz. Special thanks to the Beckham family, specifically Julie, for so generously allowing me the use of Molly's sock-swallowing habit!

'If I *was* a princess – a *real* princess,' she murmured, 'I could scatter largess to the populace. But even if I am only a pretend princess, I can invent little things to do for people. Things like this. She was just as happy as if it was largess. I'll pretend that to do things people like is scattering largess.'

A Little Princess
Frances Hodgson Burnett

Friday, January 1, Midnight, Royal Genovian Bedchamber

My New Year's Resolutions
by Princess Amelia Mignonette
Grimaldi Thermopolis Renaldo
aged 14 and 8 months

1. I will stop biting my fingernails, including the fake ones.

2. I will stop lying. Grandmere knows when I am lying anyway, thanks to my traitorous nostrils which flare every time I tell a fib, so it's not like there is even a point in trying to be less than truthful.

3. I will never veer from the prepared script while delivering televised addresses to the Genovian public.

4. I will stop accidentally saying French swear words in front of the ladies-in-waiting.

5. I will stop letting François, my Genovian bodyguard, teach me French swear words.

6. I will apologize to the Genovian Olive Growers' Association for that thing with the pits.

7. I will apologize to the Royal Chef for slipping Grandmere's dog that slice of foie gras (even though I have told the palace kitchen repeatedly that I do not eat meat).

8. I will stop lecturing the Royal Genovian Press Corps on the evils of paparrazism.

9. I will achieve self-actualization.

10. I will stop thinking so much about Michael Moscovitz.

Oh, wait. It's OK for me to think about Michael Moscovitz, BECAUSE HE IS MY BOYFRIEND NOW!!!!!!!!

MT + MM = TRUE LOVE 4-EVER

Saturday, January 2, Royal Genovian Parliament

You know, I am supposed to be on vacation. Seriously. I mean, this is my Winter Break. I am supposed to be having fun, mentally recharging for the coming semester, which is not going to be easy, as I will be moving on to Algebra II, not to mention Health and Safety class. Every other kid I know is spending his or her Winter Break in Aspen, skiing, or in Miami, getting tanned.

But me? What am *I* doing for my Winter Break?

Oh, well, right now I am just sitting in on a session of the Royal Genovian Parliament, pretending to be paying attention while these really old guys in wigs go on about whether or not to give free parking to the patrons of Genovia's many casinos.

Oh, yeah. That's a good way to spend the precious few weeks I have off from school. At this rate I will absolutely return to New York well-rested and ready for whatever awaits me in my second semester of my freshman year at Albert Einstein High School. Thanks, Dad. Thanks, Grandmere. Thanks so much.

No one even wants to hear my opinion about the whole parking thing, of course. That if we don't charge for parking it will encourage more people to drive over the French and Italian borders instead of taking the train, clogging up Genovia's already very busy streets and causing yet more strain on our infrastructure.

But why should anyone be interested in what *I* have to say on the matter? I am just the Princess of Genovia. My opinion obviously doesn't matter. Which would be why no one is listening to me, just arguing over the top of my head with my dad, who fortunately shares my opinion that a nominal parking charge – I'd jack it up to about thirty Euros a day, if I were him – is appropriate.

Fine, whatever. Like I care. I am pretending to take notes, since Grandmere told me I had to, as one day I will be sitting in my dad's chair (sadly not the throne – that is in the throne room back at the palace) in the front of Parliament and have to make all the decisions. But really I am recording my innermost thoughts and feelings in this book. Like the fact that I think Interior Minister Pepin looks exactly like this howler monkey I once saw on *World's Funniest Animals*. Or that Secretary Renard needs to start watching his saturated fats intake.

Not that it is at all princesslike to comment on the physical inadequacies of others. Especially when I have so many physical inadequacies of my own.

But it isn't like I don't have enough to worry about. I mean, I can barely bring myself to believe that a whole new year has actually started. Seriously. So much has happened to me since last year – enough that probably a better-adjusted person might have totally lost it. Fortunately, since I was born a biological freak, and am therefore very used to adversity, I was able to take it all in my stride, for the most part.

But if I had been anyone else – like Katie Holmes, or maybe one of the Olsen twins – I so fully would have not been able to deal. Because, you know, Katie and Mary Kate and Ashley are totally gorgeous and self-actualized, and never have to worry about anything. Whereas I, in less than a year's period, have been through so much trauma and angst it is a wonder I am not on *Oprah* every single day, pouring my heart out to Dr Phil. I mean, in the last four months alone, I have found out that:

1. My dad is the Prince of Genovia, and that I am his heir.
2. My grandmother is the Dowager Princess of Genovia,

4

and that it is her duty to train me for the day I will ascend the throne.

3. My mom is having my Algebra teacher's baby (but unlike me, my new brother or sister will not bear the stigma of illegitimacy, since Mom and Mr Gianini are married).

4. My best friend Lilly's brother, whom I have loved since the day I met him, when I was in the first grade and he was in fourth and he came over in the playground to give Lilly her social studies project which she had forgotten (an exact replica of the Parthenon, in red Play Doh), actually loves me back, and now we are going out.

Or at least we will when I get done with my first official visit to Genovia since discovering I am the sole heir to its throne, and am allowed to return to my normal life as a ninth-grader in New York City.

I am telling you, a lesser person would have had to check herself into Bellevue. These are extremely startling, almost earth-shattering discoveries. It is only due to the fact that so many excruciatingly horrible things have happened to me throughout my life – excessively large feet; lack of notable mammary growth; general difficulty in asserting myself in front of peers, resulting in unpopularity; owning an overweight pet cat; inability to comprehend multiplication of fractions – that I have been able to cope at all. I mean, I am way used to affliction by now.

Not that the part about Michael is an affliction. The knowledge that my love for him is not unrequited, like Wolverine's for Jean Grey in *X-MEN*, is the only bright spot in my otherwise hideous existence.

Oh, and the baby brother or sister thing. That's pretty cool, too. Though I'd prefer it if my mom would let the doctor tell her what it is she's having, so I don't have to keep writing *brother or sister* all the time. Mom says she doesn't want to know, since if it's a boy she won't push, due to not wanting to bring another Y-chromosomed oppressor into the world (Mr G says that is just the hormones talking, but I'm not so sure. My mom can be pretty anti-Y chromosome when she puts her mind to it).

I can't help wondering, as I sit here, listening to some dude whose title I don't know – although in his purple and gold sash he looks a little like Mayor McCheese – go on about the cost of parking-garage time clocks, not to mention parking-garage attendants, what lies in store for me in the coming year. I mean, last year I got:

a. a crown
b. a new stepdad
c. a potential baby brother or sister, and
d. a handsome, smart, funny boyfriend . . . my heart's one desire.

What could *possibly* happen next?

Sunday, January 3, Royal Genovian Rose Garden

Poem for M. M.

> Across the deep-blue shining sea,
> is Michael, far away from me.
> But he doesn't seem so far away —
> though I haven't seen him for sixteen days —
> because in my heart Michael stays
> and there he'll beat forever always.

OK, that poem sucks. I can see I am going to have to work harder if I am to come up with a fitting tribute to my love.

Tuesday, January 5, Royal Quarters of the Dowager Princess

Grandmere is yelling at me again.

As if I don't totally get why everybody is so mad about the whole speech thing. I mean, I have already resolved that I will never again veer from the prepared script while addressing the Genovian populace.

But why am I the only one in this country who thinks pollution is an important issue? If people are going to dock their yachts (at least cruisers are banned) in the Genovian harbour, they really ought to pay attention to what they are throwing overboard. I mean, dolphins and sea turtles get their noses stuck in those plastic six-pack holders all the time, and then they starve to death because they can't open their mouths to eat. All people have to do is snip the loops before they throw the holders out, and everything would be fine.

Well, all right, not *everything*, since you shouldn't be throwing trash overboard in the first place. That is why my dad fully had all those Grecian-urn-shaped trash receptacles placed at convenient intervals all along the pier. You would think people would consider actually using them. I mean, the sea is not their garbage can.

I cannot stand idly by while helpless sea creatures are being abused by trendy Bain de Soleil-addicts in search of that perfect St Tropez tan.

Besides, if I am to be the ruler of Genovia someday, people need to realize I am not going to be merely a figurehead – unlike *some* royals I could mention. I intend to tackle serious issues during my reign, such as the tossing of plastic six-pack holders in the bay. And the fact that all the foot traffic from the day-trippers coming off the yachts that dock in the

Genovian harbour is destroying some of our most histori-cally important bridges, such as the Pont des Vierges (Bridge of the Virgins), so named after my great-great-great-great-great-great-great grandmother Agnes, who threw herself off it rather than become a nun like her father wanted her to be. (She was all right: the Genovian royal navy fished her out and she ended up eloping with the ship's captain, much to the consternation of the house of Renaldo).

You would think people – OK, Grandmere and my dad – would recognize that it is important for me to establish my voice as heir to the throne now. Mr Gianini once told me that it is better to start off mean and get nicer as the semes-ter goes by than start nice and have everybody think they can walk all over you.

Whatever. I wish I could call Michael, or even Lilly, but I can't because they are spending Winter Break at their grandmother's in Florida and I don't even know the num-ber. They are not getting back until the day before I do! How I have survived this long, without my boyfriend and best friend to talk to, is a mystery wrapped in an enigma.

I am fully starting to hate it here. Everybody at school was all, 'Oh you are so lucky, you get to spend Christmas in a castle being waited on hand and foot . . .'

Well, believe me, there is nothing so great about living in a castle. First of all, everything in it is really old. And yeah, it's not like it was built in 500AD or whenever it was that my ancestress, Rosagunde, first became princess or whatever. But it was still built in, like, the 1600s and let me tell you what they didn't have in the 1600s:

1. Cable TV
2. DSL
3. Toilets

Which is not to say there isn't a satellite dish, but hello, this is my dad's place, the only channels he has got pro-grammed are like CNN, CNN Financial News, and the golf channel.

Where is MTV 2, I ask you? Where is the Lifetime Movie Channel for Women?

Not that it matters because I am spending all my time being run off my feet. It isn't as if I ever even get a free moment to pick up a remote and go, 'Ho hum, I wonder if there's a Tracy Gold movie on'.

No. I mean, even now I am supposed to be taking notes on Grandmere's lecture about the importance of sticking to the prepared script during televised public addresses. Like I didn't get it the first time she said it, or the nine-hundredth time, or however many times it has been since Christmas Eve, when I supposedly ruined everything with my treatise on plastic six-pack holders.

But let's say I even did get a moment to myself, and I wanted to, you know, send an email to one of my friends, or perhaps even my BOYFRIEND. Well, not so simple, because guess what, castles built in the 1600s simply aren't wired for the World Wide Web. And yeah, the Palais de Genovia audio-visual squad is trying, but you still have, like, three feet of sandstone, or whatever the palace is made out of, to bore through before you can even start installing any cable.

It is like trying to wire the Alamo.

Oh, yeah, and the toilets? Let me just tell you that back in the 1600s, they didn't know so much about sewerage. So now, four hundred years later, if you put one square too much toilet paper in the bowl and try to flush, you create a mini indoor tsunami.

Plus, the only person living here in the castle who is remotely close to my age is my cousin, Prince René, who spends inordinate amounts of time gazing at his own reflection in the back of his ceremonial sword. And technically he isn't even really my cousin anyway. Some ancestor of his was awarded a principality by the king of Italy way back in like 600AD, same as great-great-and-so-on Grandma Rosagunde. Except that René's principality no longer exists, as it was absorbed into Italy three hundred years ago.

René doesn't seem to mind, though, because everyone still calls him His Highness Prince René, and he is extended every privilege of a member of the royal household – even though his palace now belongs to a famous shoe designer, who has turned it into a resort for wealthy Americans to come for the weekend and make their own pasta and drink two-hundred-year-old balsamic vinegar.

Still, just because René is four years older than me, and a freshman at some French business school, doesn't mean he has the right to patronize me. I mean, I believe gambling is morally wrong, and the fact that Prince René spends so many hours at the roulette wheel instead of utilizing his time in a more productive fashion – such as helping to promote the protection of the nesting grounds of the giant sea turtles who lay their eggs on Genovian beaches – irks me.

So yes, I did mention this to him. It just seems to me that Prince René needs to realize there is more to life than racing around in his Alfa Romeo, or swimming in the palace pool wearing nothing but one of those little black Speedos (which are very stylish here in Europe). I also asked my dad to please, for the love of all that is holy, stick to swimming trunks, which, thankfully, he has.

And, OK, René just laughed at me.

But at least I can rest easy knowing I have done everything I could to show one extremely self-absorbed prince the error of his profligate ways.

So that's it. That is my life in Genovia. Basically, all I want is to go home. I would not even mind having to start school early if it meant I could forgo this evening's dinner with the Prince and Princess of Liechtenstein. Who are totally nice people, but hello, it's Tuesday, I could be watching *Buffy* instead.

With my new boyfriend.

My new boyfriend with whom I have not even been able to have a date yet, because the very day after we finally confessed our secret passion to one another, we were cruelly torn apart and cast to opposite sides of the earth – I to my castle in Genovia, and he to his grandmother's condo in Boca Raton.

You know, it has been exactly eighteen days since we last spoke to one another. It is entirely possible that Michael has forgotten all about me by now. I know Michael is vastly superior to all the other members of his species – boys, I mean. But everyone knows that boys are like dogs – their short-term memory is completely nil. You tell them your favourite fictional character is Xena, Warrior Princess, and next thing you know, they are going on about how your favourite fictional character is Xica of Telemundo. Boys just don't know any better, on account of how their brains are too filled up with stuff about modems and *Star Trek Voyager* and Limp Bizkit and all.

Michael is no exception to this rule. Oh, I know he is co-valedictorian of his class, and got a perfect score on his SATs and was accepted early-decision to one of the most prestigious universities in the country. But, you know, it took him about five million years even to admit he liked me. And that was only after I'd sent him all these anonymous love letters. Which turned out not to be so anonymous because he fully knew it was me the whole time thanks to all of my friends, including his little sister, having such exceptionally large mouths.

But, whatever. I am just saying, eighteen days is a long time. How do I know Michael hasn't met some other girl? Some Floridian girl, with long, sun-streaked hair, and a tan, and breasts? Who has access to the Internet and isn't cooped up in a palace with her crazy grandma, a homeless, Speedo-wearing prince and a freakish, hairless miniature poodle?

'Amelia!' Grandmere just shrieked at me. 'Are you paying attention?'

Yeah, sure, Grandmere. I'm paying attention. You are only squandering what are supposed to be the best days of my life. And probably, because of you, right now my boyfriend is strolling down the beach with some girl named Tiffany who can do long division in her head and knows how to ride a boogie board.

But yes, I am paying attention to your very boring lecture about maintaining regal poise at all times.

'I swear I do not know what is wrong with you,' Grandmere said. 'Your head has been in the clouds ever since we left New York. Even more so than usual.' Then she narrowed her eyes at me – always a very scary thing, because Grandmere has had black kohl tattooed all around her lids so that she can spend her mornings shaving off her eye-brows and drawing on new ones rather than messing around with mascara and eyeliner. 'You are not thinking about *that boy*, are you?'

That boy is what Grandmere has started calling Michael, ever since I announced that he was my reason for living. Well, except for my cat, Fat Louie, of course.

'If you are speaking of Michael Moscovitz,' I said to her, in my most regal voice, 'I most certainly am. He is never far from my thoughts, because he is my heart's breath.'

Grandmere gave a very rude snort in response to this.

'Puppy love,' she said. 'You'll get over it soon enough.'

Um, I beg your pardon, Grandmere, but I so fully will not. I have loved Michael for approximately eight years. That is more than half my life. A deep and abiding passion such as this cannot be dismissed as easily as that, nor can it be defined by your pedestrian grasp of human emotion.

I didn't say any of that out loud, though, on account of how Grandmere has those really long nails that she tends to 'accidentally' stab people with.

Except that even though Michael really is my reason for living and my heart's breath, I don't think I'll be decorating my Algebra notebook with hearts and flowers and curlicue Mrs Michael Moscovitzes, the way Lana Weinberger decorated hers (only with Mrs Josh Richters, of course). Not only because doing stuff like that is completely lame and because I do not care to have my identity subjugated by taking my husband's name, but also because as consort to the ruler of Genovia, Michael will of course have to take my name. Not Thermopolis. Renaldo. Michael Renaldo. That looks kind of nice, now that I think about it.

Thirteen more days until I see the lights of New York and Michael's dark brown eyes again. Please God, let me live that long.

HRH Michael Renaldo
  M. Renaldo, Prince Consort
    Michael Moscovitz Renaldo of Genovia

Friday, January 8, 2 a.m., Royal Genovian Bedchamber

This just occurred to me:

When Michael said he loved me that night during the Non-Denominational Winter Dance, he might have meant love in the platonic sense. Not love in the tides of flaming passion sense. You know, like maybe he loves me like a friend.

Only you don't generally stick your tongue in your friend's mouth, do you?

Well, maybe here in Europe you might. But not in America, for God's sake.

Except Josh Richter used tongue that time he kissed me in front of the school, and he was certainly never in love with me!!!!!!!!!

This is very upsetting. Seriously. I realize it is the middle of the night and I should be at least trying to sleep since tomorrow I have to go cut the ribbon at the new children's wing of the Prince Philippe Memorial Hospital.

But how can I sleep when my boyfriend – the first real boyfriend I have ever had, since my last boyfriend, Kenny, doesn't count, seeing as how I didn't actually like him as more than just a friend – could be in Florida, loving me as a friend, and, at this very minute, actually falling in love with some girl named Tiffany?

Why am I so stupid? Why didn't I demand that Michael specify when he said he loved me? Why didn't I go, 'Love me how? Like a friend? Or like a life partner?'

I am so retarded.

And even if he managed to find the phone number of the palace somehow (and if anyone could, it would be Michael, since he once figured out a way to program his computer to autodial the *700 Club*'s toll-free donation hotline every two seconds, thus costing Pat Robertson a quarter of a million dollars in a single weekend and causing him to yank the toll-free number off the air, which, in the world of computer hacking, is practically like winning a Nobel Prize) I am sure the palace operator wouldn't even put the call through. Apparently, I get something like seven hundred calls a day, none of which are from people I actually know. No, they're all from creepy paedophiles who would like to receive an autographed photo of me, or from girls who want to know what it was like when I met Prince William (he is a very cute guy and everything, but my heart fully belongs to another).

I am never going to be able to sleep now. I mean, how can I, knowing that the man I love could conceivably think of me only as a friend he likes to French kiss?

There is just one thing I can do: I have to call the only person I know who might be able to help me. And it is OK to call her because:

1. it is only six o'clock where she is, and
2. she got her own mobile phone for Christmas, so even though right now she is skiing in Aspen, I can still reach her, even if she is on a ski lift or whatever.

Thank God I have my own phone in my room. Even if I do have to dial nine to get a line outside of the palace.

Friday, January 8, 3 a.m., Royal Genovian Bedchamber

Tina answered on the very first ring! She totally wasn't on a ski lift. She sprained her ankle on a slope yesterday. Oh, thank you, God, for causing Tina to sprain her ankle, so that she could be there for me in my hour of need.

And it is OK because she says it only hurts when she moves.

Tina was in her room at the ski lodge, watching the Lifetime Movie Channel when I called (*Co-Ed Call Girl*, in which Tori Spelling portrays a young woman struggling to pay for her college education with money earned working as an escort – based on a true story).

At first it was very difficult to get Tina to focus on the situation at hand. All she wanted to know about was what Prince William was like. I tried to explain to her that, beyond commenting that it was hot on the Côte d'Azur for December, Prince William and I hardly spoke to one another; I because my heart, of course, belongs to another, and he because apparently he found my treatise on the plight of the giant sea turtle less than scintillating.

This was extremely disappointing to Tina.

'The least you could have done,' she said, 'was get his email address. I mean, even Britney Spears has that, and she's not even royalty.'

Ever since she started going out with him, Tina's boyfriend, Dave Farouq El-Abar, has shied away from commitment, saying that a man can't let himself get tied down before the age of sixteen. So, even though Tina claims Dave is her Romeo in cargo pants, she has been keeping her eyes open for a nice boy willing to make a commitment.

Although I think Prince William is too old for her. I suggested she try for Will's little brother Harry, who is actually very cute as well, but Tina said then she'd never get to be queen, a sentiment I guess I can understand, although believe me, being royal loses a lot of its glamour once it actually happens to you.

'Look,' I said. 'I'm sorry, OK? But I had other things on my mind. Like for instance that there is a distinct possibility Michael only likes me as a friend.'

'What?' Tina was shocked. 'But I thought you said he used the L word the night of the Non-Denominational Winter Dance!'

'He did,' I said. 'Only he didn't say he was *in* love with me. He just said he loved me.'

Fortunately I didn't have to explain any further. Tina has read enough romance novels to know exactly what I was getting at.

'Guys don't say the word love unless they mean it, Mia,' she said. 'I know. Dave never uses it with me.' There was a throb of pain in her voice.

'Yes, I know,' I said, sympathetically. 'But the question is, *how* did Michael mean it? I mean, Tina, I've heard him say he loves his dog. But he is not *in* love with his dog.'

'I guess I can see what you mean,' Tina said, though she sounded kind of doubtful. 'So, what are you going to do?'

'That's why I'm calling you!'

So then, just as I'd known she would, Tina came up with a plan. She was perfectly appalled when she found out Michael and I had not even spoken since the night of the Non-Denominational Winter Dance. I explained to her the whole phone situation, and she said, no problem, that I should call her back in five minutes. So I did. It was a really long five minutes, but I managed to keep from going crazy during it by pushing down all my cuticles with the tip of my sceptre, which was lying around.

Pushing down your cuticles is not biting them, so I was still well within the confines of my New Year's resolution.

When I called back precisely five minutes later, Tina had the number of Michael's grandmother's condo in Florida!

'How did you get it?' I asked her, in astonishment.

'Easy,' Tina said. 'I just called information, and asked for the number for every Moscovitz in Boca Raton, and then I called each one on the list until I got the right one. Lilly answered. She's expecting your call.'

I couldn't believe how nice this was of Tina. Also how stupid I was not to have thought of doing it myself.

'Now that you have the number,' Tina said, 'how are you going to find out? Whether Michael is in love with you or not? I mean, you're not just going to ask him, are you?'

'Well,' I said. 'Yeah. That was the plan.'

'You can't put him on the spot like that,' Tina said. 'You've got to be more subtle. Remember, he's Michael, which of course makes him vastly superior to most people, but he's still a guy.'

I hadn't thought of this. I hadn't thought of a lot of things, apparently. I couldn't believe that I had just been going along on this sea of bliss, happy just to know Michael even liked me, while the whole time he could have been falling in love with someone else.

'Well,' I said. 'Maybe I should just be like, "Do you like me as a friend, or do you like me as a girlfriend?"'

'Mia,' Tina said, 'I really do not think you should ask Michael point-blank like that. He might run away in fear, like a startled fawn. Boys have a tendency to do that, you know. They aren't like us. They don't like to talk about their feelings.'

It is just so sad that to get any kind of trustworthy advice about men, I have to call someone six thousand miles away. Thank God for Tina Hakim Baba, is all I have to say.

'So what do you think I should do?' I asked.

'Well, it's going to be hard for you to do anything,' Tina said, 'until you get back here. The only way to tell what a boy is feeling is to look into his eyes. You'll never get anything out of him over the phone. Boys are no good at talking on the phone.'

This was certainly true, if my ex-boyfriend Kenny had been any sort of indication.

'I know,' Tina said, sounding like she'd just gotten a good idea. 'Why don't you ask Lilly?'

'I don't know,' I said. 'I'd feel kind of funny about dragging her into something that's between Michael and me . . .' The truth was, Lilly and I still hadn't really even talked about me liking her brother, and her brother liking me back. I had always thought she'd be kind of mad about it. But then it turned out in the end she actually kind of helped us get together, by telling Michael I was the one who'd been sending him these anonymous love letters.

'Just ask her,' Tina said. 'And then call me back! I want to know what she says.'

'OK,' I said.

Then I hung up and looked at the number Tina had given me for Lilly and Michael's grandmother's condo. I have to admit that, as I dialled, my fingers were shaking. I mean, I was going to talk to Michael – Michael, my new boyfriend, whom I'd loved for years and years – for the first time since we'd stood kissing outside my apartment building on Thompson Street. What was I going to say? I had no idea. The only thing I knew for sure was that I was not going to say, 'Do you like me as a friend, or do you like me as a girl-friend?' Because Tina had told me not to.

Lilly answered on the first ring. Our conversation went like this:

Lilly: *(Sounding grouchy)* It's about time. I thought you'd never call.

Me: *(Sounding defensive)* You never gave me your grandma's number.

Lilly: What? And you couldn't figure it out? I mean, you take off for Genovia, and you don't leave me a number where I can reach you . . .

Me: I didn't know the number. My dad always calls me. Besides, you didn't give me the number where you were going to be, either . . .

Lilly: You don't respond to my emails . . .

Me: There's no DSL here. Only dial-up, and it takes forever, and besides, I don't know how to access my account from Europe . . .

Lilly: I even called your mom, and she gave me the number, and the stupid palace operator wouldn't put me through! She said something about Prince William. Are you two going out now, or something?

Me: *(Way surprised)* Me and Prince William? NO! I barely said two words to him. Why? *(Starting to panic)* Did the papers say I'm going out with him? Because I'm not. I'm totally not. Does Michael think I'm going out with him?

Lilly: How should I know? I'd have to talk to him.

Me: You two aren't talking? Why aren't you talking? Because he's going out with another girl? Is that it, Lilly? Michael met another girl, didn't he? Does she know how to boogie board? Oh, my God, I'm going to kill myself.

Lilly: What happens when people go to Europe, anyway? Do they suddenly become insane, or something?

Me: Just tell me the truth, Lilly, I can take it. Has Michael found another girl? Is her name Tiffany? All girls from warm states are named Tiffany.

Lilly: First of all, for Michael to have met another girl, that would mean he'd have to tear himself from his laptop and leave the condo, which he hasn't done once the entire time we have been here. He is as pasty-skinned as ever. Secondly, he is not going to go out with some girl named Tiffany, because he likes you.

Me: *(Practically crying with relief)* Really, Lilly? You swear? You aren't just lying to make me feel better?

Lilly: No, I'm not. Though I don't know why I should be so nice to you, since you didn't even remember his birthday.

I felt something clutch at my throat.

'His birthday?' I shrieked. 'Oh my God, Lilly, I completely forgot!'

'Yes,' Lilly said. 'You did. But don't worry. I'm pretty sure he didn't expect a card or anything. I mean, you're off being the Princess of Genovia. How can you be expected to remember something as important as your boyfriend's birthday?'

This seemed really unfair to me. Michael and I have only been going out for twenty-one days, and for twenty of them, I had neither seen nor spoken to him, not even once. Plus, I have been busy. I mean, it is all very well for Lilly to joke, but I haven't seen her christening any battleships or campaigning among her populace for the rights of bottlenose dolphins. It may never have occurred to anyone, but this princess stuff is hard work.

'Lilly,' I said. 'Can I talk to him, please? Michael, I mean?'

'I suppose,' Lilly said with a sigh, sounding very tired of me. Then she screamed, 'Michael! Phone!'

It was a long time after that that I finally heard some footsteps, and then Michael going to Lilly, 'Thanks,' and Lilly going, 'Whatever.' Then Michael picked up the phone and went, kind of curiously, since Lilly hadn't told him who it was, 'Hello?'

Just hearing his voice made me forget all about how it was gone two in the morning and I was miserable and hating my life. Suddenly it was like it was two in the afternoon and I was lying on one of the beaches I was working so hard to protect from erosion and pollution by tourists, with the warm sun pouring down on me and someone offering me an icy-cold Orangina from a silver tray. That's how Michael's voice made me feel.

'Michael,' I said. 'It's me.'

'Mia,' he said, sounding genuinely happy to hear from me. I don't think it was my imagination, either. He really did sound pleased, and not like he was getting ready to dump me at all. 'How are you?'

'I'm OK,' I said. Then, to get it out as soon as possible, I went, 'Listen, Michael, I can't believe I missed your birthday. I suck. I can't believe how much I suck. I am the most horrible person who ever walked the face of the planet. I should be in jail, like Winona Ryder.'

Then Michael did a miraculous thing. He laughed. Laughed! Like missing his birthday was nothing!

'Oh, that's all right,' he said. 'I know you're busy over there. And there's that time-zone thing, and all. So, how is it? How did your speech go? The one on Genovian TV? Did your crown fall off? I know you were afraid it might.'

I practically melted right there in the middle of my big fancy royal bed, with the phone clutched to my ear and

23

everything. I couldn't believe he was being so nice to me, after the terrible thing I had done. It wasn't like twenty-one days had gone by at all. It was like we were still standing in front of my stoop, with the snow coming down and looking so white against Michael's dark hair, and Lars getting mad in the vestibule because we wouldn't stop kissing and he was cold and wanted to go inside already.

I couldn't believe I had ever thought Michael might fall in love with some Floridian girl with boobs and a boogie board. I mean, I still wasn't exactly sure he was in love with me, or anything. But I was pretty sure he liked me.

And right there, at past two in the morning, sitting by myself in my royal bedchamber in the Palais de Genovia, that was enough.

So I told him about my speech, and how I'd ruined it by going off about the plastic six-pack holders, which Michael agreed was a vitally important issue. Then I told him about the sea turtles, and about my plan to organize teams of volunteers to patrol the beaches during nesting season to make sure that the eggs were not disturbed by tourists, or by the machines they bring in every morning to comb the sand and pick up all the seaweed that washes up during high tide.

And then I asked him about his birthday, and he told me how they'd gone to Red Lobster, and Lilly had an allergic reaction to her shrimp cocktail and they'd had to cut the meal short to go to Promptcare because she'd swelled up like Violet in *Willy Wonka and the Chocolate Factory*, and now she has to carry a syringe filled with adrenaline around with her in case she accidentally ingests shellfish ever again, and how Michael's parents got him a new laptop for when he goes to college and how when he gets back to New York he is thinking about starting a band since he is having trouble finding sponsors for his webzine *Crackhead* on account of how he did that ground-breaking exposé on how much Windows sucks and how he only uses Linux now.

Apparently a lot of *Crackhead*'s former subscribers are frightened of the wrath of Bill Gates and his minions.

I was so happy to be listening to Michael's voice that I didn't even notice what time it was or how sleepy I was getting until he went, 'Hey, isn't it like three in the morning there?' which by that point it almost was. Only I didn't care because I was so happy just to be talking to him.

'Yes,' I said, dreamily.

'Well, you'd better get to bed,' Michael said. 'Unless you get to sleep in. But I bet you have stuff to do tomorrow, right?'

'Oh,' I said, still all lost in rapture, which is what the sound of Michael's voice sends me into. 'Just a ribbon-cutting ceremony at the hospital. And then lunch with the Genovian Historical Society. And then a tour of the Genovian zoo. And then dinner with Minister of Culture and his wife.'

'Oh, my God,' Michael said, sounding alarmed. 'Do you have to do that kind of stuff every day?'

'Uh-huh,' I said, wishing I were there with him, so that I could gaze into his adorably brown eyes while hearing his adorably deep voice, and thus know whether or not he loved me, since this was, according to Tina, the only way you could tell with boys.

'Mia,' he said, with some urgency, 'you'd better get some sleep. You have a huge day ahead of you.'

'OK,' I said, happily.

'I mean it, Mia,' he said. He can be so authoritative sometimes, just like the Beast in *Beauty and the Beast*, my favourite Broadway show of all time. Or the way Patrick Swayze bossed Baby around in *Dirty Dancing*. So, so exciting. 'Hang up the phone and go to bed.'

'You hang up first,' I said.

Sadly, he got less bossy after this. Instead, he started talking in this voice I had only ever heard him use once before, and that was on the stoop in front of my mom's apartment building the night of the Non-Denominational Winter Dance, when we did all that kissing.

Which was actually even more exhilarating than when he was bossing me around, to be truthful.

'No,' he said. 'You hang up first.'

'No,' I said, thrilled to pieces. 'You.'

'No,' he said. 'You.'

'Both of you hang up,' Lilly said, very rudely, over the extension. 'Grandma needs to call Uncle Mort in Schenectady to see how his toe surgery went.'

So we both said goodbye very hastily and hung up.

But I'm almost positive Michael would have said 'I love you' if Lilly hadn't been on the line.

Saturday, January 9, 2 p.m., Royal Genovian Limo

Grandmere can be so mean. Seriously. Imagine pinching me, just because she thought I had dozed off for a few seconds at lunch! I swear I am going to have a bruise now. It's a good thing I don't have any time to go to the beach, because if I did and anyone saw the scar she'd left, they'd probably call the Genovian Child Protection Services.

And I'm sorry, but the Genovian Historical Society was really, really boring. Worse than the FOIL system, practically. How many times can you hear about marauding Visigoths, anyway?

And I wasn't asleep, either. I was just resting my eyes.

Grandmere says it is thoughtless of Michael to keep me up all hours whispering sweet nothings in my ear. I informed her very firmly that Michael had actually told me to hang up, because he cares very deeply about me, and that I was the one who kept on talking. And that we don't whisper sweet nothings to one another, we have substantive discussions about art and literature and Bill Gates's stranglehold on the software industry.

To which Grandmere replied, *'Pfuit!'* which is French for Big Deal.

But you can tell she is totally jealous because she would like a boyfriend who is as smart and thoughtful as mine. But that will so never happen, because Grandmere is too mean, and besides, there is that whole thing she does with her eyebrows. Boys like girls with real eyebrows, not painted-on ones.

Saturday, January 9, 10 p.m., Royal Genovian Bedchamber

I am so excited! Tina, not being able to join her family on the ski slopes, spent all day in an Aspen Internet café looking up all of her friends' horoscopes. She just faxed over my and Michael's astrological chart! I am taping it here in my journal so I won't lose it. It is so accurate it is making my spine tingle.

Michael — Date of Birth = January 5:

Capricorn is the leader of the Earth signs. Here is a stabilizing force, one of the hardest-working signs of the Zodiac. The Mountain Goat has intense powers of self-concentration, but not in an egotistical sense. Members of this sign find a great deal more confidence in what they do than in who they are. Capricorn is one very high-achiever! Without balance, however, Capricorn can become too rigid, and focus too much on achievement. Then they forget the little joys in life. When the Goat finally relaxes and enjoys life, his or her most delightful secrets emerge. No one has a better sense of humour than the Capricorn. Oh, that Cap might let us bask in that warm smile!

Mia — Date of Birth = May 1:

Ruled by loving Venus, Taurus has great emotional depth. Friends and lovers rely on the warmth and emotional accessibility of the Bull. Taurus represents consistency, loyalty and patience. Fixed Earth can be very rigid, too cautious to take some of the risks necessary in life. Sometimes the Bull ends up temporarily stuck in the mud. He or she may not want to rise to every challenge or potential. And stubborn? Ah yes! The Taurus Bull may always surface. This sign's Yin energy can also go too far, causing Taurus to become very, very passive. Still, you cannot ask for a better lover, or more loyal friend.

Courageous, ambitious Earth signs, Taurus and Capricorn seem to be made for each other. Both value career success and share a love of beauty and of lasting, classical foundations. Capricorn's irony charms the Bull, while the latter's expert sensuality rescues the Capricorn from his or her obsession with career. They enjoy talking together, and communication is excellent. They confide in each other, promising never to offend or betray the other. This could be a perfect couple.

See! We're perfect for each other! But expert sensuality? *Me?* Um, I don't think so.

Still . . . I'm so happy! Perfect! You can't get better than perfect!

Sunday, January 10, 10 a.m., Palais de Genovia Chapel

Oh, my God, I have only been Michael's girlfriend for twenty-three days, and already I suck at it. The girlfriend thing, I mean. I can't even figure out what to get him for his birthday. He is the love of my life, the reason my heart beats. You would think I would know what to get the guy.

But God no. I haven't got a clue.

Tina says the only appropriate thing to get for a boy you have only been officially dating for less than four weeks is a sweater. And she says even that is pushing it as Michael and I have not even been out on an official date yet, so technically, how can we be dating?

But a *sweater*? I mean, that is so unromantic. It is the kind of thing I would get my dad – if he wasn't so in need of anger-management manuals, which is what I got for him for Christmas. I would get a sweater for my stepdad for sure.

But my *boyfriend*?

I was kind of surprised Tina would suggest something so banal, as she is basically the resident romance expert of our little group. But Tina says the rules about what to give boys are actually very strict. Her mom told them to her. Tina's mom used to be a model and international jet-setter who once dated a sultan, so I guess she would know. The rules for presents for guys, according to Mrs Hakim Baba, go:

Length of Time Going Out:	*Appropriate Gift:*
1–4 months	Sweater
5–8 months	Cologne
9–12 months	Cigarette lighter*
1 year +	Watch

*Mrs Hakim Baba says that for a non-smoker, an engraved pocket knife or brandy flask may be substituted.

But this is better at least than Grandmere's list of what is appropriate to give boyfriends, which she presented to me yesterday, as soon as I mentioned to her my horrible faux pas of missing Michael's birthday. Her list goes:

Length of Time Going Out:	Appropriate Gift:
1–4 months	Candy
5–8 months	Book
9–12 months	Handkerchief
1 year +	Gloves

Handkerchiefs? Who gives handkerchiefs any more? Handkerchiefs are completely unhygienic!

And candy? For a *guy*????

But Grandmere says the same rules apply for girls as for boys. Michael is not allowed to give me anything but candy or possibly flowers for my birthday, either!

Overall, I think I prefer Mrs Hakim Baba's list.

Still, this whole dating/present-giving thing is so difficult! Everybody says something different. Like I called my mom and asked her what I should give Michael, and she said silk boxer shorts.

But I can't give Michael UNDERWEAR!!!!!!!

I wish my mom would hurry up and have this baby already so she would stop acting so weird. She is pretty much useless to me in her current state of hormonal imbalance.

Out of desperation, I asked my dad what I should get Michael, and he said a pen, so Michael could write to me while I am in Genovia, instead of my calling him all the time and running up a huge phone bill.

Whatever, Dad. Like anyone writes with a pen any more. And hello, I am only going to be in Genovia for

Christmas and summers, as per our agreement drawn up last September.

A pen. I am so sure. Am I the only person in my family with a modicum of romance in my bones?

Oops, gotta stop writing, Father Christoff is looking this way. But it is his own fault. I wouldn't write in my journal during mass if his sermons were even semi-inspiring. Or at least in English.

Monday, January 11, 1 a.m., Royal Genovian Bedchamber

I just got off the phone with Michael. I *had* to call him. It wasn't like I had a choice. I had to find out what he wanted for his birthday. I mean, I have to get him something. And it has to be something *really* good, since I forgot. About his birthday, and all.

Of course he says he doesn't want anything, that I am the only thing he needs (!!!!!!!!!!!) and that he will see me in eight days, and that is the best present anyone could get him.

This seems to indicate that he might actually be in love with me, as opposed to only loving me as a friend. I will, of course, have to check with Tina to see what she thinks, but I would have to say that in this case, Signs Point to Yes!!!!!!

But of course he is only saying that. That he doesn't want anything for his birthday, I mean, I have to get him *something*. Something really good. Only what?

Anyway, I really did have a reason to call him. I didn't do it just because I wanted to hear the sound of his voice, or anything. I mean, I am *not* that far gone.

Oh, all right, maybe I am. How can I help it? I have only been in love with Michael since, like, forever. I love the way he says my name. I love the way he laughs. I love the way he asks my opinion, like he really cares what I think – God knows, nobody around here feels that way. I mean, make a suggestion – like that it might save water to turn off the fountain in front of the palace at night, when no one is around anyway – and everybody practically acts like one of the suits of armour in the Grand Hall started talking.

Well, OK, not my dad. But I see him less here in Genovia than I do back home, practically, because he is so caught up

33

in parliamentary meetings, and racing his yacht in regattas, and hanging out with the new blonde bareback rider from the Cirque du Soleil – which just got to town for an extended stint at one of the casinos.

Anyway, I like talking to Michael. Is that so wrong? I mean, he is my boyfriend, after all.

So we were just saying goodbye after having had a perfectly pleasant conversation about his birthday and the Genovian Olive Growers' Association and Michael's band that he hasn't formed yet, and whether it is off-putting to call it Frontal Lobotomy, and I was just working up the guts to go, 'I miss you,' or 'I love you,' thus leaving an opening for him to say something similar back to me and therefore resolve the does-he-just-love-me-like-a-friend-or-is-he-in-love-with-me dilemma once and for all, when I heard Lilly in the background, demanding to talk to me.

Michael went, 'Go away!' but Lilly kept on shrieking, 'I have to talk to her, I just remembered I have something really important to ask her.'

Then Michael went, 'Don't tell her about that,' and my heart skipped a beat because I thought Lilly had all of a sudden remembered that Michael had been going out with some girl named Tiffany behind my back after all. Before I could say another word, Lilly had wrestled the phone away from him (I heard Michael grunt, I guess in pain because she must have kicked him or something), and then she was going, 'Oh, my God, I forgot to ask. Did you see it?'

'Lilly,' I said, since even five thousand miles away, I could feel Michael's pain – Lilly kicks hard, I know. I have been the recipient of quite a few kicks of hers over the years. 'I know that you are used to having me all to yourself, but you are going to have to learn to share me with your brother. Now, if this means we are going to have to set boundaries in our relationship, then I guess we will have to. But you can't just go around ripping the phone out of Michael's hand when he might have had something really important to—'

'Have you been watching Dr Phil again?' Lilly wanted to know. 'I can't believe they have *Oprah* there, but not email. Anyway, shut up about my sainted brother for a minute. Did . . . you . . . see . . . it?'

'See what? What are you talking about?' I thought maybe somebody had tried to jump into the polar bear cage at the Central Park Zoo again. As if those bears don't have enough problems, what with the stress of living in Manhattan and not on an iceberg, the way they are supposed to, plus being on display twenty-four/seven, weirdos are always trying to dive in there with them.

I totally don't blame those bears for ripping the arms off the last guy who tried it.

'Oh, just the movie,' Lilly said. 'Of your life. Or hadn't you heard your life story has been made into a movie of the week?'

I wasn't very surprised to hear this. There are already four unauthorized biographies about me floating around out there. One of them made the best-seller list for about half a second.

'So?' I said. I was kind of mad at Lilly. I mean, she'd booted Michael off the phone just to tell me about some dumb movie?

'Hello,' Lilly said. 'Movie. Of your life. You were portrayed as shy and awkward.'

'I *am* shy and awkward,' I reminded her.

'They made your grandmother all kindly and sympathetic to your plight,' Lilly said. 'It was the grossest mischaracterization I've seen since *Shakespeare in Love* tried to

35

pass off the Bard as a hottie with a six-pack and a full set of teeth.'

'That's horrible,' I said. 'Now can I please finish talking to Michael?'

'You didn't even ask how they portrayed me,' Lilly said, accusingly, 'your loyal best friend.'

'How did they portray you, Lilly?' I asked, looking at the big fancy clock on top of the big fancy marble mantelpiece over my big fancy bedroom fireplace. 'And make it quick, I've got a breakfast and then a ride with the Genovian Equestrian Society in exactly seven hours.'

'They portrayed me as less than fully supportive of your royalness,' Lilly practically screamed into the phone. 'They made out like after you first got that stupid haircut, I mocked you for being shallow and a trend-follower!'

'Yeah,' I said, waiting for her to get to the point of her tirade. Because, of course, Lilly hadn't been very supportive of my haircut, or my royalness – at least at first.

But it turned out Lilly had already gotten to the point of her tirade.

'I was never unsupportive of your royalness!' she shrieked into the phone, causing me to hold the receiver away from my head in order to keep my eardrums intact. 'I was your number one most supportive friend through the whole thing!'

This was so patently untrue, I thought Lilly was joking. But then I realized when she greeted my laughter with stone-cold silence that she was totally serious. Apparently Lilly has one of those selective memories, where she can remember all the good things she did, but none of the bad things. Kind of like a politician.

Because, of course, if it were true that Lilly had been so supportive of me, I never would have become friends with Tina Hakim Baba, whom I only started sitting with at lunch

36

back in October because Lilly wasn't speaking to me, on account of the whole princess thing.

'I sincerely hope,' Lilly said, 'that you are laughing in disbelief over the idea that I was ever anything less than a good friend to you, Mia. I know we've had our ups and downs, but any time I was ever hard on you, it was only because I thought you weren't being true to yourself.'

'Um,' I said, getting serious fast. 'OK.'

'I am going to write a letter,' Lilly went on, 'to the studio that produced that piece of libellous trash, demanding a written apology for their irresponsible screenwriting. And if they do not provide one – and publish it in a full-page ad in the *New York Times* – I will sue. I don't care if I have to take my case to the Supreme Court. Those Hollywood types think they can throw anything they want to in front of a camera and the viewing public will just lap it up. Well, that might be true for the rest of the proles, but *I* am going to fight for more honest portrayals of actual people and events. The man is not going to keep *me* down!'

I asked Lilly what man, thinking she meant the director or something, and she just went, 'The man! The *man*!' like I was mentally challenged, or something.

Then Michael got back on the phone and explained that 'the man' is a figurative allusion to authority, and that in the way that Freudian analysts blame everything on 'the mother', blues musicians have historically blamed their woes on 'the man'. Traditionally, Michael informed me, 'the man' is white, financially successful, in his mid to late forties, and in a position of considerable power over others.

We discussed calling Michael's band The Man, but then dismissed it as having possible misogynistic undertones.

Eight days until I can once again be in Michael's arms. Oh, that the hours would fly as fleetly as winged doves!

I just realized – Michael's description of The Man sounds a lot like my dad! Although I doubt all those blues musicians were talking about the Prince of Genovia. As far as I know, my dad has never even been to Memphis.

Monday, January 11, 2 p.m., Dowager Princess's Private Terrace

Just when it seems like maybe, just maybe, things might be starting to go my way, something always has to come along to ruin it.

And, as usual, this time it was Grandmere.

I guess she could tell, because I was so sleepy again today, that I'd been up all night talking to Michael. So this morning, between my ride with the Genovian Equestrian Society and my meeting with the Genovian Beachfront Development Society, Grandmere sat me down and gave me a lecture. This time it wasn't about the socially acceptable gifts to give a boy on his birthday. Instead, it was about Appropriate Choices.

'It is all very well and good, Amelia,' Grandmere said, 'for you to like *that boy*. But I do not think it wise of you to allow your affection for this Michael fellow to blind you to other, more suitable consorts such as—'

I interrupted to tell Grandmere that if she said the words Prince William I was going to jump off the Pont des Vierges.

Grandmere told me not to be more ridiculous than I already am. I could never marry Prince William anyway on account of his being Church of England. However, there are apparently other, infinitely more suitable romantic partners for a princess of the royal house of Renaldo than Michael. And Grandmere said she would hate for me to miss the opportunity to get to know these other young men, just because I think I have to be faithful to Michael. She assured me that, were the circumstances reversed, and Michael were the heir to a throne and a considerable fortune, she highly doubted he would be as scrupulously faithful as I was being.

I objected to this assessment of Michael's character very much. I informed Grandmere that in every aspect of Michael's life, from his being editor in chief of the now defunct *Crackhead*, to his role as treasurer in the Computer Club, he has shown nothing but the utmost loyalty and integrity. I also explained, as patiently as I could, that it hurt me to hear her saying anything negative about a man to whom I have pledged my heart.

'That is just it, Amelia,' Grandmere said, rolling her scary eyes. 'You are entirely too young to pledge your heart to anyone. I think it very unwise of you, at the age of fourteen, to decide with whom you are going to spend the rest of your life.'

I informed Grandmere that I will be fifteen in four months, and also that Juliet was fourteen when she married Romeo. To which Grandmere replied, 'And that relationship turned out very nicely, didn't it!'

Grandmere clearly has never been in love. Furthermore, she has no appreciation whatsoever of fine literature.

'And in any case,' Grandmere added, 'if you hope to keep *that boy*, you are going about it all wrong.'

I thought it was very unsupportive of Grandmere to be suggesting that I, after only having had a boyfriend for twenty-four days, during which time I had seen him exactly once, was already in danger of losing him, and said so.

'Well, I'm sorry, Amelia,' Grandmere said. 'But I can't say you know what you're about if it's true you actually want to keep this young man. You call him at all hours of the night—'

'Actually,' I said, 'where he is, it is a perfectly civilized time

40

for me to call, right after he and his grandparents and sister get back from their Early Bird special dinner.'

But Grandmere wasn't listening.

'You do not give him any reason to doubt your affections,' she went on.

'Of course not,' I said, horrified. 'Why would I do that? I love him!'

'But you mustn't let him know that!' Grandmere looked ready to throw her mid-morning Sidecar at me. 'Are you completely dense? *Never* let a man be sure of your affections for him! You did a very good job at first, with the business of forgetting his birthday. But now you are ruining everything by calling all the time. If *that boy* realizes how you really feel, he will stop trying to please you.'

'But Grandmere.' I was way confused. 'You married Grandpa. Surely he figured out you loved him if you went ahead and married him.'

'Grandpere, Mia, please, not this vulgar Grandpaw you Americans insist upon.' Grandmere sniffed and looked insulted. 'Besides which, your grandfather most certainly did not "figure out" my feelings for him. I made quite certain he thought I was only marrying him for his money and title. And I don't think I need to point out to you that we had forty blissful years together. And without separate bedrooms,' she added, with some malice, 'unlike some royal couples I could mention.'

'Wait a minute.' I stared at her. 'For forty years you slept in the same bed as Grandpere, but you never once told him that you loved him?'

Grandmere drained what was left of her Sidecar and laid an affectionate hand on top of her miniature poodle Rommel's head. Since returning to Genovia, most of Rommel's fur has started to grow back. According to the royal Genovian vet, the allergy that caused it all to fall out was to New York City in general. White fuzz was starting to come out all over him, like down on a baby chicken. But it didn't make him look any less repulsive.

'That,' Grandmere said, 'is precisely what I am telling you. I kept your grandfather on his toes, and he loved every minute of it. If you want to keep this Michael fellow, I suggest you do the same thing. Stop this business of calling him every night. Stop this business of not looking at any other boys. And stop this obsessing over what you are going to get him for his birthday. *He* should be the one obsessing over what he is going to buy to keep *you* interested, not the other way around.'

'*Me?* But my birthday isn't until May!' I didn't want to tell her that I had already figured out what I was getting for Michael. I didn't want to tell her because I had sort of snitched it out of the back of the Palais de Genovia museum.

Well, nobody else was using it, so I don't see why I can't. I'm the Princess of Genovia, after all. I own everything in that museum anyway. Or at least the royal family does.

'Who says a man should give a woman gifts only on her birthday?' Grandmere was looking at me like she pretty much despaired of me as a *Homo sapiens*. She held up her wrist. Dripping from it was a bracelet Grandmere wears a lot, one with diamonds big as European one cent pieces hanging off it. 'I got this from your grandfather on March 5, 1967. Why? March fifth is not my birthday, nor is it any kind of holiday. Your grandfather gave it to me on that day merely because he thought that the bracelet, like myself, was exquisite.' She lowered her hand back down to Rommel's head. 'That, Amelia, is how a man ought to treat the woman he loves.'

All I could think was poor Grandpa. He couldn't have

had any idea what he was getting himself into when it came to Grandmere, who'd been a total babe back when she was young, before she'd gotten her eyeliner tattooed and plucked out all her eyebrows. I'm sure Gramps just took one look at her across that dance floor where they met back when he was just the dashing heir to the throne and she was a pert young debutante, and froze, like a deer caught in headlights, never suspecting what lay ahead . . .

Years of subtle mind games and Sidecar shaking.

'I don't think I can be like that, Grandmere,' I said. 'I mean, I don't want Michael to give me diamonds. I just want him to ask me to the prom.'

'Well, he won't do it,' Grandmere said, 'if he doesn't know there's a possibility you're entertaining offers from other boys.'

'Grandmere!' I was shocked. 'I would never to go to the prom with anybody but Michael!' Not like there was a big chance of anybody else asking me, either, but I felt that was beside the point.

'But you must never let him know that, Amelia,' Grandmere said, severely. 'You must keep him always in doubt of your feelings, always on his toes. Men enjoy the hunt, you see, and once their quarry has been taken, they tend to lose all interest. Here. This is for you to read. I believe it will adequately illustrate my point.'

And then from her Gucci bag, Grandmere drew out a book, which she handed to me. I looked down at it incredulously.

'*Jane Eyre*?' I couldn't believe it. 'Grandmere, no offence, but I saw the movie and it was way boring.'

'Movie?' Grandmere said, with a sniff. 'Read that book, Amelia, and see if it doesn't teach you a thing or two about how men and women relate to one another.'

43

'Grandmere,' I said, not sure how to break it to her that she was way behind the times. 'I think people who want to know how men and women relate to one another are reading *Men Are from Mars, Women Are from Venus* these days.'

'*Read it!*' Grandmere yelled, so loudly that she scared Rommel clear off her lap. He slunk off to cower behind a potted geranium.

I swear I don't know what I did to deserve a grandmother like mine. Lilly's grandma totally worships her boyfriend, Boris Pelkowski. She is always sending him Tupperware tubs of kreplach and stuff. I don't know why I have to get a grandma who is already trying to get me to break up with a guy I've only been going out with for twenty-four days.

Seven days, twenty-three hours and forty-five minutes until I see him again.

Tuesday, January 12, 10 a.m., Session of Genovian Parliament

Jane Eyre v. boring, so far nothing but orphanages, bad haircuts and a lot of coughing.

Tuesday, January 12, 2 p.m., Still in a Session of Genovian Parliament

Jane Eyre looking up. She has gotten a job as a governess in the house of very rich guy, Mr Rochester. Mr Rochester v. bossy, much like Wolverine, or Michael.

Tuesday, January 12, 5 p.m., *Still* Sitting in on Session of Genovian Parliament

Mr Rochester = total hottie. Going on my list of Totally Hot Guys between Hugh Jackman and that Bosnian dude from *ER*.

Tuesday, January 12, 7 p.m., Ivory Dining Room

Jane Eyre = total idiot! It was not Mr Rochester's fault! Why is she being so mean to him?

Wednesday, January 13, 3 a.m., Royal Genovian Bedchamber

OK, I guess I understand what Grandmere was getting at with this book. But seriously, that whole part where Mrs Fairfax warns Jane not to get too chummy with Mr Rochester before the wedding was just because back in those days there was no birth control. Well, and also the part about him already having a wife.

Still – and I may have to consult with Lilly on this – I am pretty sure it is unwise to pattern one's behaviour on the advice of a fictional character, especially one from a book written in 1846.

However, I do get the general gist of Mrs Fairfax's warning, which was this: Do not chase boys. Chasing boys can lead to horrible things like mansions going up in flames, hand amputations and bigamous marriages. Have some self-respect and don't let things go too far before the wedding day.

Which in modern parlance translates to Don't Put Out Until Senior Prom.

I get this. I so get this.

But what is Michael going to think if I just stop calling???? I mean, he might think I don't like him any more!!!!

I guess that is Grandmere's point. I guess you are supposed to keep boys on their toes this way.

I don't know. But it seemed to work with Grandpa. And for Jane, in the end. I guess I could give it a try.

But it won't be easy. It is nine o'clock at night in Florida right now. Who knows what Michael is doing? He might have gone down to the beach for a stroll and met some beautiful, homeless musician girl, who is living under the boardwalk and making a living off the tourists, for whom she plays wryly observant folk songs on her Stratocaster. She could be wearing fringy things and be all busty and snaggletoothed, like Jewel. No boy could be expected just to walk on by when a girl like that is standing there.

No. Grandmere and Mrs Fairfax are right. I've got to resist. I've got to resist the urge to call him. When you are less available, it drives men wild, just like in *Jane Eyre*.

Though I think changing my name and running away to live with distant relations like Jane did might be going a bit too far.

Five days, ten hours, and fifty-eight minutes until I see him again.

Thursday, January 14, 11 p.m., Royal Genovian Bedchamber

Tina spent all day yesterday reading *Jane Eyre* as per my recommendation and agrees with me that there might be something to the whole letting-boys-chase-you-as-opposed-to-you-chasing-them thing. So she has decided not to email or call Dave first.

Lilly, however, refuses to take part in this scheme, as she says game-playing is for children and that her relationship with Boris is one that cannot be qualified by modern-day psycho-sexual mating practices. According to Tina (I can't call Lilly because Michael might pick up the phone and then he'll think I'm chasing him), Lilly says that *Jane Eyre* was one of the first feminist manifestos, and, though she doesn't feel that she needs Jane's brilliant guidance, she heartily approves of us using it as a model for our romantic relationships. Although she sent a warning to me through Tina that I shouldn't expect Michael to ask me to marry him until after he's gotten at least one post-graduate degree as well as a start-up position with a company that pays two hundred thousand dollars or more a year, plus an annual performance bonus.

Lilly also added that the one time she saw him ride a horse, Michael looked way unromantic, so I shouldn't get my hopes up that he's going to be jumping any stiles like Mr Rochester any time soon.

But I find this hard to believe. I am sure Michael would look very handsome on a horse.

Tina mentioned that Lilly is still upset about the movie of my life they showed the other day. Tina saw it, though, and said it wasn't as bad as Lilly is making it out to be. She said the lady who played Principal Gupta was hilarious.

But Tina wasn't in the movie, on account of her dad having found out about it beforehand and threatening the filmmakers with a lawsuit if they mentioned his daughter's name anywhere. Mr Hakim Baba worries a lot about Tina getting kidnapped by a rival oil sheikh. Tina says she wouldn't mind being kidnapped, though, if the rival oil sheikh was cute and willing to commit to a long-term relationship and remembered to buy her one of those diamond heart pendants from Kay Jewelers on Valentine's Day.

Tina says the girl who played Lana Weinberger in the movie did a fabulous job and should get an Emmy. Also that she didn't think Lana was going to be too happy about how she was portrayed, as a jealous wannabe.

Also the guy who played Josh was a babe. Tina is trying to find his email address.

Tina and I vowed that if either of us ever felt like calling our boyfriends, instead we would call one another. Unfortunately, I have no mobile so it is not like Tina will be able to reach me if I am in the middle of knighting someone or anything. But I am fully going to hit my dad up for a StarTAC phone tomorrow. Hey, I am heir to the throne of an entire country. At the very least I should have a beeper.

Note to self: look up word *stile*.

Four days, fourteen hours and forty minutes until I see Michael again.

Friday, January 15, Royal Genovian Limo on the Way to State Dinner in Neighbouring Monaco

To Do Before Leaving Genovia:

1. Find a safe place to put Michael's present where it will NOT be found by grandmother or nosy ladies-in-waiting while packing my stuff (inside toe of combat boot? Inside panties I'll be wearing on plane?)

2. Say goodbye to kitchen staff, and thank them for all the vegetarian entrées.

3. Make sure harbourmaster has hung pair of scissors off every buoy in bay for use of yachting tourists who didn't bring along their own set to snip six-pack holders.

4. Take funny nose and glasses off the statue of Grandmere in the Portrait Hall before she notices.

5. Give Rommel's mink sweater back.

6. Break François' record of eleven feet, seven inches sock-sliding down Crystal Hallway.

7. Let all the doves in the Palace dovecote go (if they want to come back, that is fine, but they should have the option to be free).

8. Let Tante Jean Marie know that this is the twenty-first century and that she no longer has to live with the stigma of feminine facial hair, and leave her my Jolene.

9. Go to the beach, just once, and walk barefoot through that famous white sand I haven't gotten within ten yards of the entire time I've been here. Also, establish Sea-Turtle Nest Patrol so that eggs will be protected.

10. Get crown fixed (combs keep spearing me in the head).

Saturday, January 16, 11 p.m. Royal Genovian Bedchamber

Grandmere so needs to get a life.

Tonight was the royal ball – you know, to celebrate the end of my first official trip to Genovia in my capacity as heir to the throne.

Anyway, Grandmere's been going on about this ball all week, like this is going to be my big chance to redeem myself for the whole snip-your-plastic-six-pack-holder thing I pulled during my first televised address to the populace.

So she makes this big deal out of my dress (a Sebastiano design – my dad finally forgave Sebastiano for putting those pictures of me wearing his designs in the *New York Times* Sunday supplement. My dad even forgave Grandmere for letting Sebastiano do it without clearing it through him first. Though things are still a little strained between the two of them – I heard him tell her to 'lay off' the other day when she was giving him grief about his latest girlfriend, one of those bendy trapeze girls from the Cirque du Soleil. I don't know what happened to the bareback rider.

And she makes this big deal out of my hair (growing out and so becoming triangle-shaped again, but who cares, boys are supposed to like girls with long hair better than girls with short hair – I read that in French *Cosmo*). And she makes this big deal out of my fingernails (OK, so in spite of the whole New Year's resolution thing, I still keep biting them. So sue me. I can't help that I am orally fixated, the man is keeping me down).

Then, after all this big-deal making, we finally get to the stupid ball. And it turns out that all that fuss was just so that Grandmere could shove me at Prince René, of all people, and the two of us could dance in front of this *Newsweek* reporter who is in Genovia to do a story on our country's transition to the Euro!

Afterwards I was all, 'Grandmere, I am willing to cool it with the calling Michael stuff, but that does not mean I am going to start going out with Prince René,' who, by the way, asked me if I wanted to step outside on to the terrazzo and have a smoke.

I, of course, told him I do not smoke and that he shouldn't either as tobacco is responsible for half a million deaths a year in the United States alone, but he only laughed at me all James Spader from *Pretty in Pink*-ishly.

So then I told him not to get any big ideas, that I already have a boyfriend and that maybe he didn't see the movie of my life, but I fully know how to handle guys who are only after me for my crown jewels.

So then Prince René said I was adorable, and I said please don't patronize me as I am not a child, and then my dad came up and asked me if I had seen the Prime Minister of Greece and I said, 'Dad, Grandmere is trying to fix me up with René,' and then my dad got all tight-lipped and took Grandmere aside and had A Word with her while Prince René slunk off to go make out with one of the Hilton sisters.

Afterwards, Grandmere came up and told me not to be so ridiculous, that she merely wanted Prince René and I to dance together because it was a nice photo op for *Newsweek* and that maybe if they ran a story on us, it would attract more tourists.

To which I replied that in light of our crumbling infrastructure more tourists is exactly what this country doesn't need.

I suppose if my palace had been bought out from under me by some shoe designer, I would be pretty desperate, too, but I wouldn't hit on a girl who has the weight of an entire populace on her shoulders, and already has a boyfriend, besides.

On the bright side, if *Newsweek* does run the photo, maybe Michael will get all jealous of René the way Mr Rochester did of that St John guy, and he'll boss me around some more!!!

Two days, fourteen hours, and twelve minutes until I see Michael again.

I CAN'T WAIT!!!!!!!!!!!!!!!

Monday, January 18, 3 p.m., Genovian Time, Royal Genovian Jet, 20,000 Feet in the Air

I cannot believe that:

a. my dad is staying in Genovia in order to resolve the parking crisis rather than coming back to New York with me

b. he actually believed Grandmere when she said that my princess lessons need to continue

c. she (not to mention Rommel) is coming back to New York with me

IT IS NOT FAIR. I held up my part of the agreement. I went to every single princess lesson Grandmere gave last fall. I passed Algebra. I gave my stupid address to the Genovian people.

Grandmere says that in spite of what I might think, I still have a lot to learn about governance. Except that she is so wrong. I know she is only coming back to New York with me so she can go on torturing me. It is kind of like her hobby now.

It is so not fair.

And yes, before I left, my dad slipped me a hundred dollars and told me if I didn't make a fuss about Grandmere, he'd make it up to me someday.

But there is nothing he can do to make *this* up to me. Nothing.

He says she is just a harmless old lady and that I should try to enjoy her while I can because someday she won't be with us any more. I just looked at him like he was crazy. Even he couldn't keep a straight face. He went, 'OK, I'll donate two hundred bucks a day to Greenpeace if you keep her out of my hair.'

Which is funny because of course my dad hasn't got any. Hair, I mean.

I sincerely hope Greenpeace appreciates the supreme sacrifice I am making for its sake.

So she is coming back to New York with me, and dragging a cowering Rommel along with her. Just when his fur had started to grow back, too. Poor thing.

I told my dad I'd put up with the whole princess lesson thing again this semester, but that he'd better get one thing straight with Grandmere beforehand, and that is this: I have a serious boyfriend now. Grandmere had better not try to sabotage this, or think she can be trying to fix me up with any more Prince Renés. I don't care how many royal titles the guy has, my heart belongs to Michael Moscovitz, Esquire.

My dad said he'd see what he could do. But I don't know how much he was actually paying attention, since Tapeka, the bareback rider, and Natasha, the trapeze artist, were kind of having a fight over him at the time in the royal palace lemon grove.

Anyway, a little while ago I told Grandmere myself that she better watch it where Michael is concerned.

'I don't want to hear anything more about how I'm too young to be in love,' I said, over the lunch (poached salmon for Grandmere, three-bean salad for me) we were served by the royal Genovian flight attendants. 'I am old enough to know my own heart, and that means I am old enough to give that heart away if I choose to.'

Grandmere said something about how then I should get ready for some heartache, but I ignored her. Just because her romantic life since Grandpa died has been less than satisfactory is no reason for her to be so cynical about mine. I mean, that is just what she gets for going out with media moguls and dictators and stuff.

Michael and I, on the other hand, are going to have a great love, just like Jane and Mr Rochester. Or Buffy and Angel. Or Brad and Jennifer.

Or at least, we will if we ever actually get to go out on a date.

Twenty-two hours until I see him again.

Monday, January 18, Martin Luther King Day, National Holiday, the Loft, at Last

I am so happy I feel like I could burst, just like that eggplant I once dropped out of Lilly's sixteenth-floor bedroom window.

I'm home!!!!!!! I'm finally home!!!!!!

I cannot tell you how good it felt to look out the window of the plane and see the bright lights of Manhattan below me. It brought tears to my eyes, knowing I was once again in the air space over my beloved city. Below me, I knew, cab drivers were running down little old ladies (unfortunately not Grandmere); deli owners were short-changing their customers; investment bankers were not cleaning up after their dogs; and people all over town were having their dreams of becoming a singer, actress, musician, novelist, or dancer completely crushed by soulless producers, directors, agents, editors and choreographers.

Yes, I was back in my beautiful New York. I was back home at last.

I especially knew it when I stepped off the plane, and there was Lars, waiting for me, ready to take over bodyguarding duty from François, the guy who had looked after me in Genovia, and who had taught me all the French swear words. Lars looked especially menacing on account of being all darkly tanned from his month off. He had spent his Winter Break with Tina Hakim Baba's bodyguard, Wahim, snorkelling and hunting wild boar in Belize. He gave me a piece of tusk as a memento of his trip, even though of course I don't approve of killing animals recreationally, even wild boars, who really can't help being so ugly and mean.

Then, sixty-five minutes later, thanks to a pile-up on the Long Island Expressway, I was home.

It was so good to see my mom!!!!! She is beginning to show now. I didn't want to say anything because even though my mom says she does not believe in the Western standard of idealized beauty and thinks that there is nothing wrong with a woman who is bigger than a size eight, I'm pretty sure that if I had said anything like, 'Mom, you're huge,' even in a complimentary fashion, she would start to cry. After all, she still has more than four months left to go.

So instead I just went, as I tried to hug her close even though her belly is starting to get in the way, 'That baby has to be a boy. Or if it's not it's a girl who is going to be as tall as me.'

'Oh, I hope so,' my mom said, as she brushed tears of joy from her face – or maybe she was crying because Fat Louie was biting her ankles so hard in his effort to get near me. 'I could use another you for when you aren't around. I missed you so much! There was no one to berate me for ordering roast pork and wonton soup from Number One Noodle Son.'

'I tried,' Mr Gianini assured me.

Mr G looks great, too. He is growing a goatee beard. I pretended I liked it.

Then I bent down and picked up Fat Louie, who was yowling to get my attention, and gave him a great big hug. I may be wrong, but I think he lost weight while I was away. I do not want to accuse anyone of purposely starving him, but I noticed his dry-food bowl was not completely full. In fact, it was perilously close to being only half full. I always keep Fat Louie's bowl filled to the brim, because you never know when there might be a sudden plague, killing everyone in Manhattan but cats. Fat Louie can't pour out his own food, having no thumbs, so he needs a little extra just in case we all die and there is no one around to open the bag for him.

But the loft looks so great!!!!!!!! Mr Gianini did a lot to it while I was gone. He got rid of the Christmas tree – the first time in the history of the Thermopolis household that the Christmas tree was out of the loft by Easter – and had the place wired for DSL. So now you can email or go on the Internet anytime you want, without tying up the phone.

It is like a Christmas miracle.

And that's not all. Mr G also fully redid the darkroom, leftover from when my mom was going through her Ansel Adams stage. He pulled the boards off the windows and got rid of all the noxious chemicals that have been sitting around since forever because my mom and I were too afraid to touch them. Now the darkroom is going to be the baby's room! It is so sunny and nice in there. Or at least it was until my mom started painting the walls with scenes of important historical significance, such as the trial of Julius and Ethel Rosenberg and the assassination of Martin Luther King, so that, she says, the baby will have an understanding of all the problems facing our nation (Mr G assured me privately that he is going to paint over the whole thing as soon as my mom gets admitted to the maternity ward. She will never know the difference once the endorphins kick in. All I can say is thank God Mom picked a man with so much common sense with whom to reproduce this time around).

But the best thing of all was what was waiting for me on the answering machine. My mom played it for me proudly almost the minute I walked through the door.

IT WAS A MESSAGE FROM MICHAEL!!!! MY FIRST MESSAGE FROM MICHAEL SINCE I BECAME HIS GIRLFRIEND!!!!!!!!!!!!!

Which of course means it worked. The my-not-calling-him thing, I mean.

The message goes like this:

'Uh, hi, Mia? Yeah, it's Michael. I was just wondering if you could, uh, call me when you get this message. 'Cause I haven't heard from you in a while. And I just want to know if you're, uh, OK. And make sure you got home all right. And that there's nothing wrong. OK. That's all. Well. Bye. This is Michael, by the way. Or maybe I said that. I can't remember. Hi, Mrs Thermopolis. Hi, Mr G. OK. Well. Call me, Mia. Bye.'

I took the tape out of the message machine and am keeping it in the drawer of my nightstand along with:

a. some grains of rice from the bag Michael and I sat on at the Cultural Diversity Dance, in memory of the first time we ever slow-danced together

b. a dried-out piece of toast from the *Rocky Horror Show*, which is where Michael and I went on our first date, though it wasn't really a date because Kenny came too

c. a cut-out snowflake from the Non-Denominational Winter Dance, in memory of the first time Michael and I kissed

It was the best Christmas present I could ever have had, that message. Even better than DSL.

So then I came into my room and unpacked and played the message over about fifty times on my tape player, and my mom kept coming in to give me more hugs and asking me if I wanted to listen to her new Liz Phair CD and wanting to show me her stretch marks. Then, about the thirtieth time she came in, I was playing Michael's message again, and she was all, 'Haven't you called him back yet, honey?' and I went, 'No,' and she went, 'Well, why not?' and I went, 'Because I am trying to be like Jane Eyre.'

And then my mom got all squinty-eyed like she does whenever they are debating funding for the arts in Congress.

'Jane Eyre?' she echoed. 'You mean the book?'

'Exactly,' I said, tugging the little Napoleonic diamond napkin holders that the Prime Minister of France had given me for Christmas out from beneath Fat Louie. He had lain down inside my suitcase, I guess in the mistaken belief that I was packing, not unpacking, and he wanted to try to stop me from going away again. 'See, Jane didn't chase boys, she let them chase her. And so Tina and I, we've both taken solemn vows that we are going to be just like Jane.'

My mom, unlike Grandmere had been, didn't look happy to hear this.

'But Jane Eyre was so mean to poor Mr Rochester,' she cried.

I didn't mention that this was what I had thought, too . . . at first.

'Mom,' I said, very firmly. 'I think you're forgetting the whole first-wife-in-the-attic thing.'

'Because she was a lunatic,' my mom pointed out. 'It wasn't like they had psychotropic drugs back then. Keeping Bertha locked in the attic was kinder, really, than sending her to a mental hospital, considering what they were like during that era, with people chained to the walls and the whole no TV thing. Really, Mia. I swear I don't know where you get half your ideas. Jane Eyre? Who told you about Jane Eyre?'

'Um,' I said, stalling because I knew my mom wasn't going to like the answer. 'Grandmere.'

My mom's lips got so thin, they completely disappeared.

'I should have known,' she said. 'Well, Mia, I think it is commendable that you and your friends have decided not to chase boys. However, if a boy leaves a nice message on the answering machine like Michael did, it could hardly be construed as chasing for you to do the polite thing and return his call.'

I thought about this. My mom was probably right. I mean, it isn't as if Michael has a crazy wife in the attic. The Fifth Avenue apartment where the Moscovitzes live doesn't even have an attic, so far as I know.

'OK,' I said, setting down the clothes I'd been putting away. 'I guess I could return his call.' My heart was swelling at the very idea. In a minute – less than a minute, if I could get my mom out of my room fast enough – I'd be talking to Michael! And there wouldn't be that weird swooshing sound there always is when you call from across the ocean. Because there was no ocean separating us! Just Washington Square Park. 'Returning calls probably doesn't count as chasing. That would probably be OK.'

My mom, who was sitting on the end of my bed, just shook her head.

'Really, Mia,' she said. 'You know I don't like to contradict your grandmother . . .' This was the biggest lie I'd heard since the Prince of Liechtenstein told me I waltzed divinely, but I let it slide, on account of Mom's condition. '. . . but I really don't think you should be playing mind games with boys. Particularly a boy you care about. Particularly a boy like Michael.'

'Mom, if I want to spend the rest of my life with him, I have to play games with Michael,' I explained to her, patiently. 'I certainly can't tell him the truth. If he were ever to learn the depths of my passion for him, he'd run like a startled fawn.'

My mom looked stunned. 'A what?'

'A startled fawn,' I explained. 'See, Tina told her

boyfriend Dave Farouq El-Abar how she really feels about him, and he pulled a total David Caruso on her.'

My mom blinked. 'A who?'

'David Caruso,' I said. I felt sorry for my mom. Clearly she had only managed to snag Mr Gianini by the skin of her teeth. I couldn't believe she didn't know this stuff. 'You know, he disappeared for a really long time. Dave only resurfaced when Tina managed to scrounge Wrestlemania tickets for the Garden. And ever since, Tina says things have been really awkward.' Done unpacking, I shooed Fat Louie out of the suitcase, closed it, and put it on the floor. Then I sat next to my mom on the bed. 'Mom,' I said. 'I do *not* want that to happen to me and Michael. I love Michael more than anything in the entire world, except for you and Dad and Fat Louie.'

I just said the you and Dad part to be polite. I think I love Michael more than I love my mom and dad. It sounds terrible to say, but I can't help it, it is just how I feel.

But I will never love anyone or anything as much as I love Fat Louie.

'So don't you see?' I said to her. 'What Michael and I have, I don't want to mess it up. He's my Romeo in black jeans.' Even though of course I have never seen Michael in black jeans. But I am sure he has some. It is just that we have a dress code at our school, so usually when I see him he is in grey flannel pants, as that is part of our uniform.

It seemed to take my mom a minute to digest all this. When she had, all she said was, 'I respect that you want to take things with Michael slowly, Mia. But I do think that if you haven't seen a boy in a month, and he leaves a message for you, the decent thing to do is to call him back. If you don't, I think you can pretty much guarantee he is going to run. And not like a startled fawn, either.'

I blinked at my mom. She had a point. I saw then that Grandmere's scheme – you know, of always keeping the man you love guessing as to whether or not you love him back – had some pitfalls. Such as, he could just decide you don't like him, and take off, and maybe fall in love with some other girl of whose affection he could be assured, like Judith Gershner, president of the Computer Club and all-round prodigy, even though supposedly she is dating a boy from Trinity, but you never know, that could be a ruse to lull me into a false sense of security about Michael and put my guard down, thinking he is safe from Judith's fruit-fly-cloning clutches . . .

'Mia,' my mom said, looking at me all concerned. 'Are you all right?'

I tried to smile, but I couldn't. How, I wondered, could Tina and I have overlooked this very serious flaw in our plan? Even now, Michael could be on the phone to Judith, or some other equally intellectual girl, talking about quasars or photons or whatever it is smart people talk about.

'Mom,' I said, standing up. 'You have to go. I have to call him.'

I was glad the panic that was clutching my throat wasn't audible in my voice.

'Oh, Mia,' my mom said, looking pleased. 'I really think you should. Charlotte Brontë is, of course, a brilliant author, but you've got to remember, she wrote *Jane Eyre* back in the 1840s, and things were a little different then.'

'Mom,' I said. Lilly and Michael's parents, the Drs Moscovitz, have this totally hard and fast rule about calling after eleven on schoolnights. It is *verboten*. And guess what, it was practically eleven. And my mom was still standing there, keeping me from having the privacy I would need if I were going to make this all-important call.

'Oh,' she said, smiling. Even though she is pregnant, my mom is still somewhat of a babe, with all this long black hair that curls just right. Clearly I had inherited my dad's hair, which I've actually never seen, since he's always been bald since I've known him.

DNA is so unfair.

Anyway, FINALLY she left – pregnant women move SO slowly, I swear you would think evolution would have made them quicker so they could get away from predators or whatever, but I guess not – and I lunged for the phone, my heart pounding because at last, AT LAST, I was going to get to talk to Michael, and my mom had even said that it was all right, that my calling him wouldn't count as chasing since he'd called me first . . .

. . . and just as I was about to pick up the receiver, the phone rang. My heart actually did this flippy thing inside my chest, like it does every time I see Michael. It was Michael calling, I just knew it. I picked up after the second ring – even though I didn't want him dumping me for some more attentive girl, I didn't want him to think I was sitting by the phone waiting for him to call, either – and said, in my most sophisticated tone, 'Hello?'

Grandmere's cigarette-ravaged voice filled my ear. 'Amelia?' she rasped. 'Why do you sound like that? Are you coming down with something?'

'Grandmere.' I couldn't believe it. It was ten fifty-nine! I had exactly one minute left to call Michael without running the risk of the wrath of his parents. 'I can't talk now. I have to make another call.'

'Pfuit!' Grandmere made her traditional noise of disapproval. 'And who would you be calling at this hour, as if I didn't know?'

'Grandmere.' Ten fifty-nine and a half. 'It's OK. He

69

called me first. I am returning his call. It is the polite thing to do.'

'It's too late for you to be calling *that boy*,' Grandmere said.

Eleven o'clock. I had missed my opportunity. Thanks to Grandmere.

'You'll see him at school tomorrow, anyway,' she went on. 'Now, let me speak to your mother.'

'My mother?' I was shocked by this. Grandmere never talks to my mom, if she can help it. They haven't gotten along since my mom refused to marry my dad after she got pregnant with me, on account of her not wanting her child to be subjected to the vicissitudes of a progenitive aristocracy.

'Yes, your mother,' Grandmere said. 'Surely you've heard of her.'

So I went out and passed the phone to my mom, who was sitting in the living room with Mr Gianini, watching *Absolutely Fabulous*. I didn't tell her who was on the phone, because if I had, my mom would have told me to tell Grandmere that she was in the shower, and then I would have had to talk to her some more.

'Hello?' my mom said, all brightly, thinking it was one of her friends calling to comment on the high jinks of Eddie and Patsy. I slunk out as fast I could. There were several heavy objects lying around the couch that my mom could have hurled in my direction if I'd stayed within missile range.

Back in my room, I tried to figure out what to do about Michael. What was I going to say to him tomorrow, when Lars and I pulled up in the limo to pick up him and Lilly before school? That I'd gotten in too late to call? What if he noticed my nostrils flaring as I spoke? I don't know if he's figured out that they do that when I lie, but I think I'd sort of mentioned it to Lilly, since I have a complete inability to keep my mouth shut about stuff I really should just keep to myself, and supposing she told him?

Then, as I sat there dejectedly on my bed, pretty sleepy because in Genovia it was five in the morning, I had a brilliant idea. I could see if Michael was logged on, and instant message him! I could do it even though my mom was on the phone with Grandmere, because we have DSL now!

So I scrambled over to my computer and did just that. And he was online!

Michael, I wrote. Hi, it's me! I'm home! I wanted to call you, but it's after eleven, and I didn't want your mom and dad to get mad.

Michael has changed his screen name since the demise of *Crackhead*. Now he's no longer CracKing. He's LinuxRulz.

LinuxRulz: Welcome home! It's good to hear from you. I was worried you were dead or something.

So he had noticed I'd stopped calling! Which meant the plan that Tina and I had come up with was working perfectly. At least, so far.

FtLouie: No, not dead. Just super-busy. You know, fate of the aristocracy resting on my shoulders and all of that. So should Lars and I pick you and Lilly up for school tomorrow?

>

```
LinuxRulz: That'd be good. What are you doing
          Friday?
```

What am I doing Friday? Was he asking me out? Were Michael and I actually going to have a date? At last????

I tried to type casually so he wouldn't know that I was so excited. I had already freaked Fat Louie out by jumping up and down in my computer chair and almost rolling over his tail.

```
FtLouie:   Nothing, so far as I know. Why?
>
LinuxRulz: Want to go to dinner at the Screening
           Room? They're showing the first Star
           Wars. You know the real first one, not
           that waste of digital pixels, The
           Phantom Headcase.
```

OH MY GOD HE WAS ASKING ME OUT. Dinner and a movie. At the same time, because at the Screening Room you sit at a table and eat dinner while the movie is going. And *Star Wars* is only my favourite movie of all time, after *Dirty Dancing*. Could there BE a girl luckier than me? No, I don't think so.

My fingers were trembling as I wrote:

```
FtLouie:   I think that would be OK. I'll have to
           check with my mom. Can I let you know
           tomorrow?
>
LinuxRulz: OK. So see you tomorrow? Around 7.45?
>
FtLouie:   Tomorrow, 7.45.
```

I wanted to add something like I miss you or I love you, but I don't know, it just felt too weird, and I couldn't do it. I mean, it's embarrassing, telling the person you love that you love them. It shouldn't be, but it is. Also, it didn't seem like something Jane Eyre would do. Unless, you know, she had just discovered the man she loved had gone blind in a heroic attempt to rescue his crazy firebug wife from an inferno she'd set herself.

Asking me out to dinner and a movie didn't really seem the same, somehow.

Then Michael wrote:

```
LinuxRulz: Kid, I've been from one side of this
           galaxy to the other . . .
```

which is one of my favourite lines from the first *Star Wars*. So then I wrote:

```
FtLouie:   I happen to like nice men . . .
```

jumping ahead to *The Empire Strikes Back*, to which Michael replied:

```
LinuxRulz: I'm nice.
```

Which is better than saying I love you, because right after Han Solo says that, he totally kisses her. OH MY GOD!!! It really is like Michael is Han Solo and I'm Princess Leia, because Michael is good at fixing stuff like hyper drives, and, well, I'm a princess, and I'm very environmentally conscious like Leia, and everything.

Plus Michael's dog Pavlov sort of looks like Chewbacca, if Chewbacca were a sheltie.

73

I could not imagine a more perfect date if I tried. Mom will let me go, too, because the Screening Room isn't that far away, and it's *Michael*, after all. Even Mr Gianini likes Michael, and he doesn't like many of the boys who go to Albert Einstein, as he says they are mostly all walking bundles of testosterone.

I will never get to sleep now, I am too worked up. *I am going to see him in eight hours and fifteen minutes.*

And on Friday I am going to be sitting next to him in a darkened room. All alone. With no one else around. Except all the waitresses and the other people at the movie.

The Force is *so* with me.

Tuesday, January 19, First Day of School after Winter Break, Homeroom

I barely made it out of bed this morning. In fact, the only reason I was able to drag myself out from beneath the covers – and Fat Louie, who lay on my chest purring like a lawnmower all night long – was the prospect of seeing Michael for the first time in thirty-two days.

It is completely cruel to force a person of my tender years, when I should be getting at least nine hours of sleep a night, to travel back and forth between two such drastically different time zones, with not even a single day of rest in-between. I am completely jet lagged, and I am sure it is going to stunt not only my physical growth (not in the height department because I am tall enough, thank you, but in the mammary gland division, glands being very sensitive to things like disrupted sleep cycles), but my intellectual growth as well.

And now that I am entering the second semester of my freshman year, my grades are actually going to start to matter. Not that I intend to go to college or anything, at least not right away. I, like Prince William, want to take a year off between high school and college, hopefully volunteering for Greenpeace in one of those boats that goes out between Japanese and Russian whaling ships and the whales. I don't think Greenpeace takes volunteers who don't have at least a 3.0 average.

Anyway, it was murder getting up this morning, especially when, after I'd dragged on my school uniform, I realized my Queen Amidala panties weren't in my underwear drawer. I have to wear my Queen Amidala underwear on the first day of every semester, or I'll have bad luck for the rest of the year. I *always* have good luck when I wear my Queen Amidala panties. For instance, I was wearing them the night of the Non-Denominational Winter Dance, when Michael finally told me he loved me.

I have to wear them on the first day of second semester, just like I'll have to send them to the laundry-by-the-pound place and get them washed before Friday so I can wear them on my date with Michael. Because I'm going to need extra good luck that night, since I plan on giving Michael his birthday present then. His birthday present that I'm hoping he'll like so much, he'll fall in love with me, if he isn't already. I am still not too clear on that whole point.

So I had to go into my mom's room, the one she shares with Mr Gianini, and wake her up and be all, 'Mom, where's my Queen Amidala underwear?' Thank God Mr G was in the shower. I swear to God if I'd had to see them in bed together in the condition I was in at that time, I'd have gone completely Anne Heche.

My mom, who sleeps like a log even when she isn't pregnant, just went, 'Shurnowog,' which isn't even a word.

'Mom,' I said. 'I need my Queen Amidala panties. Where are they?'

But all my mom said was, 'Kapukin.'

So then I got an idea. Not that I really thought there was any way my mom wasn't going to let me go out with Michael, after her uplifting speech about him the night before. But just to make sure she couldn't back out of it, I went, 'Mom, can I go with Michael for dinner and a movie at the Screening Room this Friday night?'

And she went, rolling over, 'Yeah, yeah, scuniper.'

So I got that taken care of.

But I still had to go to school in my regular underwear,

which creeped me out a little because there's nothing special about it, it is just boring and white.

But then I kind of perked up when I got in the limo, because of the prospect of seeing Michael and all.

But then I was like, Oh, my God, what was going to happen when I saw Michael? Because when you haven't seen your boyfriend in thirty-two days, you can't just be all, 'Oh, hi,' when you see him. You have to, like, give him a hug or *something*.

But how was I going to give him a hug in the car? With Lars watching? I mean, at least I wasn't going to have to worry about my stepdad watching, since Mr G fully refuses to take the limo to school with me and Lars and Lilly and Michael every morning, even though we are all going to the same place. But Mr Gianini says he likes the subway. He says it is the only time he gets to listen to music he likes (Mom and I won't let him play Blood, Sweat and Tears in the loft, so he has to listen to it on his Diskman).

But what about Lilly? I mean, Lilly was totally going to be there. How can I hug Michael in front of Lilly? And OK, it is partly because of Lilly that Michael and I ever got together in the first place. But that does not mean that I feel perfectly comfortable participating in, you know, public displays of affection with him *right in front of her*.

If this were Genovia it would be all right to kiss him on either cheek, because that is the standard form of greeting there.

But this is America, where you barely even shake hands with people, unless you're like the mayor.

Plus there was the whole Jane Eyre thing. I mean, Tina and I had resolved we were not going to chase our boyfriends, but we hadn't said anything about how to greet them again after not having seen them for thirty-two days.

I was almost going to ask Lars what he thought I ought to

do when I had a brainstorm right as we were pulling up to the Moscovitzes' building. Hans, the driver, was going to hop out and open the door for Lilly and Michael, but I went, 'I've got it,' and then *I* hopped out, instead.

And there was Michael, standing in the slush, looking all tall and handsome and manly, the wind tugging at his dark hair. Just the sight of him set my heart going about a thousand beats per minute. I felt like I was going to melt . . .

. . . especially when he smiled once he saw me, a smile that went all the way up to his eyes, which were as deeply brown as I remembered, and filled with the same intelligence and good humour that had been there the last time I had gazed into them, thirty-two days ago.

What I could not tell was whether or not they were filled with love. Tina had said I'd be able to tell, just by looking into his eyes, whether or not Michael loved me. But the truth is, all I could tell by looking into his eyes was that Michael doesn't find me utterly repulsive. If he had, he'd have looked away, the way I do when I see that boy in the cafeteria at school who always picks the corn out of his chilli.

'Hi,' I said, my voice suddenly super-squeaky.

'Hi,' Michael said, his voice not squeaky at all, but really very thrillingly deep and Wolverine-like.

So then we stood there with our gazes locked on one another, and our breath coming out in little puffs of white steam, and people hurrying down Fifth Avenue on the sidewalk around us, people I barely saw. I hardly even noticed Lilly go, 'Oh, for Pete's sake,' and stomp past me to climb into the limo.

Then Michael went, 'It's really good to see you.'

And I went, 'It's really good to see you, too.'

From inside the limo Lilly went, 'It's really cold out, will you two hurry up and get in here already?'

So then I went, 'I guess we'd better . . .'

And Michael went, 'Yeah,' and put his hand on the limo door to hold it open for me. But as I started to duck in there, he put his other hand on my arm, and when I turned around to see what he wanted (even though I kinda already knew) he went, 'So can you go, on Friday night?'

And I went, 'Uh-huh.'

And then he kind of pulled on my arm in a very Mr Rochester-like manner, causing me to take a step towards him, and faster than I'd ever seen him move before, he bent down and kissed me, right on the mouth, in front of his doorman and all the rest of Fifth Avenue!

I have to admit, Michael's doorman and all of the people passing by, including everyone on the M1 bus that went barrelling down the street at that very moment, didn't seem to take very much notice of the fact that the Princess of Genovia was getting kissed right there in front of them.

But *I* noticed. *I* noticed, and it felt great. It made me feel like maybe all my worrying about whether Michael loved me as a potential life partner as opposed to just as a friend had maybe been stupid.

Because you don't kiss a friend like that.

So then I slid into the back of the limo with Lilly, a big silly smile on my face that I was totally afraid she might make fun of, but I couldn't help it, I was so happy. Because in spite of not having on my Queen Amidala underwear, I was already having a good semester, and it wasn't even fifteen minutes old!

Then Michael got in beside me and closed the door, and Hans started to drive and Lars said, 'Good morning,' to Lilly and Michael and they said 'Good morning' back and I didn't even notice that Lars was smirking behind his latte until Lilly told me later.

'Like,' she said, 'we didn't all know what you were doing out there.'

But she said it in a nice way.

I was so happy, I hardly even heard what Lilly was talking about on our way to school, which was the whole movie thing. She had sent, she said, a registered letter to the producers of the movie of my life, but still had received no response, even though it was now over a week.

'It is,' Lilly said, 'just another example of how those Hollywood types think they can get away with whatever they want. Well, I'm here to tell them they can't. If I don't hear back from them by tomorrow, I'm going to the news media.'

That got my attention. I blinked at her. 'You mean you're going to have a press conference?'

'Why not?' Lilly shrugged. 'You did it, and up until recently, you could barely formulate a coherent sentence in front of a camera. So how hard can it be?'

Wow. Lilly is really mad about this movie thing. I guess I'm going to have to watch it myself to see how bad it is. If Tina is anything to go by, the other kids at school don't seem to have thought much about it. But then they were all in St Moritz or their winter homes in Ojai when it came on. They were too busy skiing or having fun in the sun to watch any stupid made-for-TV movie about the life of one of their classmates.

From the look of the number of casts people are wearing – Tina was by far not the only one to sprain something on her vacation – everyone had a much better time on their break than I did. Even Michael says he spent most of the time at his grandparents' condo sitting on the balcony and writing songs for his new band.

I guess I am the only one who passed the whole of my

break sitting in parliamentary sessions, trying to negotiate parking rates for casino garages in downtown Genovia.

Still, it's good to be back. It's good to be back because for the first time in my whole entire academic career, the guy I like actually likes – maybe even loves – me back. And I get to see him between classes and in Gifted and Talented fifth period—

Oh, my God! I totally forgot! It is a new semester! They are assigning us all new schedules! They are passing them out at the end of Homeroom, after the announcements. What if Michael and I aren't in the same Gifted and Talented class any more? I am not even supposed to be in Gifted and Talented at all, seeing as how I am neither. They only put me in there when it became clear I was flunking Algebra, so I have an extra period for independent study. I was supposed to be in Tech. Ed. for that period. TECH. ED.! WHERE THEY MAKE YOU BUILD SPICE RACKS!

Second semester is Domestic Arts. IF I GET PUT IN DOMESTIC ARTS THIS SEMESTER INSTEAD OF GIFTED AND TALENTED I WILL DIE!!!!!!

Because I ended up getting a B minus in Algebra last semester. They don't give you independent study periods if you are making B minuses. B minus is considered good. Except, you know, to Greenpeace.

Oh, God, I knew it. I just KNEW something bad was going to happen if I didn't wear my Queen Amidala under-wear.

So, if I'm not in G and T, then the only time I will see Michael will be at lunch and between classes. Because he is a senior, and I am only a freshman, so it's not like I'll be in advanced calculus with him, or that he'll be in French 2 with me.

81

And I might not even be able to see him at lunch! We could conceivably not have the same lunch periods!

And even if we do, what is the likelihood that Michael and I are even going to sit together at lunch? Traditionally I have always sat with Lilly or Tina, and Michael has always sat with the Computer Club and upperclassmen. Is he going to come sit by me now? No way can I go sit at *his* table. All those guys over there ever do is talk about things I don't understand, like plasma screens and how easy it is to hack into India's missile defence system . . .

Oh, God, they are passing out the new class schedules now. Please don't let me be in Domestic Arts. PLEASE

Tuesday, January 19, Algebra

HA! My Queen Amidala underwear might be missing, but the power of the Force is with me nonetheless. My class schedule is EXACTLY the same as last semester's, except that by some miracle I now have Bio. third period instead of World Civ. (Oh, God, please don't let Kenny, my former Bio. partner and ex-boyfriend, have been switched to third period Bio., too). World Civ. is now seventh. And instead of PE fourth period, we all have Health and Safety.

And no Tech. Ed. or Domestic Arts, thank GOD!!!!! I don't know who told the administration that I am gifted and talented, but whoever it was, I am eternally grateful, and I will definitely try to live up to it.

I also happen to know that not only does Michael still have fifth period G and T, but he has the same lunch hour as I do, too. I know that because after I got here to Algebra and had sat down and got out my notebook (I always seem to remember all my notebooks on the first day of the semester. It is just the rest of the year I forget them) and my Algebra I–II textbook, Michael came in!

Yes, he came right into Mr G's second semester freshman Algebra class, like he belonged there, or something, and everyone was staring at him, including Lana Weinberger, because you know seniors don't generally just go walking into freshman classes, unless they are working for the attendance office and bringing someone a hall pass or something.

But Michael doesn't work for the attendance office. He popped into Mr G's class just to see *me*. I know because he came right up to my desk with his class schedule in his hand and went, 'What lunch have you got?' and I told him, 'A,' and he said, 'Same as me. You have G and T after?' and I said, 'Yes,' and he said, 'Cool, see you at lunch.'

Then he turned around and walked out again, looking all tall and collegiate with his Jansport backpack and New Balances.

And the way he said, 'Hey, Mr G,' all casually to Mr Gianini – who was sitting at his desk with a cup of coffee in his hands and his eyebrows all raised – as he went walking out.

Well, you just can't get cooler than that.

And he had been in here to see me. ME, MIA THER-MOPOLIS. Formerly the most unpopular person in the entire school, with the exception of that guy who doesn't like corn in his chilli.

So now everyone who had not seen Michael and me kissing at the Non-Denominational Winter Dance knows that we are going out, because you don't walk into someone else's classroom between periods to look at their schedule unless you are dating.

I could feel all the gazes of my fellow Algebra sufferers boring into me, including Lana Weinberger's, even as the bell was ringing. You could practically hear everybody going, '*He*'s going out with *her*?'

And I guess it *is* a little hard to believe. I mean, even *I* can hardly believe it's true. Because of course it's common knowledge that Michael's the third best-looking boy in the whole school, after Josh Richter and Justin Baxendale (though if you ask me, having seen Michael plenty of times without a shirt on, he makes those other guys look like that Quasimodo dude), so what is he doing with *me*, a biological freak with feet the size of skis and no breasts to speak of and nostrils that flare when I lie?

Plus I am a lowly freshman, and Michael is a senior who has already been accepted early-decision to an Ivy League school right here in Manhattan. Plus Michael is co-valedictorian of his class, being a straight-A student, whereas I barely scraped by Algebra I. Plus Michael is way involved with extra-curriculars, including the Computer Club, Chess Club and Physics Club. He designed the school's website. He can play, like, ten instruments. And now he is starting his own band.

Me? Yeah. I'm a princess.

And that's about it.

And that's only *recently*. Before I found out I was a princess, I was just this massive reject who was flunking Algebra and always had orange cat-hair all over her school uniform.

So yeah, I guess you could say that a lot of people were kind of surprised to see Michael Moscovitz come striding up to my desk in Algebra to compare class schedules. I could feel them all staring at me after he left and the bell rang, and I could hear them buzzing about it among themselves. Mr G tried to bring everybody to order, going, 'OK, OK, break's over. I know it's been a long time since you last saw one another, but we've got a lot to tackle in the next nine weeks,' only of course nobody paid any attention to him but me.

In the desk in front of me, Lana Weinberger was already on her mobile – the new one that I'd paid for, on account of my having stomped her old one to bits in a semi-psychotic fit last month – going, 'Shel? You are not going to *believe* what just happened. You know that freaky girl in your Latin class, the one with the TV show and the flat face? Yeah, well, her brother was just in here comparing class schedules with Mia Thermopo—'

Unfortunately for Lana, Mr Gianini has a thing about mobile usage during class time. He fully pounced on her, snatched her phone away, put it up to his ear and said, 'Ms

Weinberger can't speak to you right now as she is busy writing a thousand-word essay on how rude it is to make mobile phone calls during class time,' after which he threw her phone in his desk drawer and told her she'd get it back at the end of the day, once she'd handed in her essay.

I wish Mr G would give Lana's mobile phone to me, instead. I would fully use it in a more responsible manner than she does.

But I guess even if the teacher is your stepdad, he can't just confiscate things from other students and give them to you.

Which is a bummer because I could really use a mobile phone right now. I just remembered I never asked my mom what Grandmere wanted when she called last night.

Oh, crud. Integers. Gotta go.

B = (x : x is an integer such that x > 0)

Defn: When integer is squared the result is called a perfect square

Tuesday, January 19th, Health and Safety

This is so boring – MT

You're telling me. How many times in our academic careers are they going to tell us having unprotected sex can result in unwanted pregnancy and AIDS? Do they think it didn't soak in the first five thousand times or something? – LM

Apparently. Hey, did you see Mr Wheeton open the door to the teachers' lounge, look at Mademoiselle Klein, then leave? He is so obviously in love with her.

I know, you can slightly tell, he is always bringing her lattes from Ho's. What is THAT about, if not luv? Wahim will be devastated if they start going out.

Yeah, but why would she choose Mr Wheeton over Wahim? Wahim has all those muscles. Not to mention a gun.

Who can explain the vagaries of the human heart. Not I. Oh, my God, look, he's moving on to vehicular safety. Could this BE more boring? Let's make a list. You start it.

OK.

Mia Thermopolis's *New and Improved* List of Hottest Guys

(with commentary by Lilly Moscovitz):

1. Michael Moscovitz *(obviously cannot agree due to genetic link to said individual. Will concede he is not hideously deformed)*
2. Ioan Gruffud from the *Horatio Hornblower* series *(agreed. He can shiver me timbers anytime he wants)*
3. The guy who plays Clark Kent in *Smallville (duh – only they should have him join the school swimming team because he needs to take his shirt off more per episode)*
4. Hayden Christiansen *(again, duh. Ditto swimming team. There must be one for Jedis. Even ones who have embraced the Dark Side)*
5. Mr Rochester *(fictional character, but will agree he exudes certain rugged manliness)*
6. Patrick Swayze *(um, not. So not. What is WRONG with you????)*
7. Captain von Trapp from *The Sound of Music (another fictional character, but the captain is a hottie extraordinaire. I would pit him against the Nazi horde anytime)*
8. Justin Baxendale *(duh. I heard an eleventh-grader tried to kill herself because he looked at her. Seriously. Like his eyes were so hypnotic, she went full-on Sylvia Plath. She is in counselling now)*
9. Heath Ledger *(oooh, in the rock and roll knight movie, totally. Not so much* The Patriot, *though, I found his performance in that film somewhat stilted. Plus he never took his shirt off).*
10. Beast from *Beauty and the Beast (I think I know someone else who needs counselling)*

Tuesday, January 19th, Gifted and Talented

I am so depressed.

I know I shouldn't be. I mean, everything in my life is going so great:

Great Thing Number One:

The boy I have been madly in love with my entire life, practically, loves, or at least really likes, me back, and we are going out on our first real date on Friday.

Great Thing Number Two:

I know it is only the first day of the new semester, but as yet I am not flunking anything, including Algebra.

Great Thing Number Three:

I am no longer in Genovia, the most boring place on the entire planet with the possible exception of Algebra, and Grandmere's princess lessons.

Great Thing Number Four:

I don't have Kenny for my Bio. partner any more. My new partner is Shameeka – what a relief. Which I know is cowardly (feeling relieved that I don't have to sit by Kenny any more), but I am pretty sure Kenny thinks I am this horrible person to have led him on, like, all those months, when really I liked someone else (only thankfully not the person Kenny THOUGHT I liked. I still can't believe Kenny dumped me because he thought I was in love with Boris Pelkowski). Anyway, the fact that I don't have to deal with any hostile looks from Kenny's direction (even though he fully has a new girlfriend, a girl from our Bio. class, as a matter of fact – *he* didn't waste any time) is probably really going to boost my grade in that class. Plus Shameeka is really good at science, on account of her being a Pisces.

Great Thing Number Five:
I have really cool friends who seem actually to want to hang around with me, and not just because I am a princess, either.

But that, see, is the problem. I have all these great things going for me, and I should be totally happy. I should be over the moon with joy.

And maybe it's only the jet lag talking – I am so tired, I can barely keep my eyes open – or maybe it's PMS – I am sure my internal clock is way messed up from all this intercontinental flying. But I can't shake this feeling that I am . . .

Well, a total reject.

And I will tell you why I feel this way. I mean, take Gifted and Talented class, for example:

WHAT AM I DOING IN HERE????

I am not gifted. I am not talented. I am not good at anything. Really. I have no gifts or special talents. I AM A POSER. I SHOULD NOT BE HERE.

It hit me today at lunch. I was sitting there like always with Lilly and Boris and Tina and Shameeka and Ling Su, and then Michael came and sat down with us, which of course caused this total cafeteria sensation, since seniors NEVER sit at the freshman tables.

And I was totally embarrassed but of course proud and pleased, too, because Michael NEVER sat at our table back when he and I were just friends, so his sitting there MUST mean that he is at least slightly in love with me, because it is quite a sacrifice to give up the intellectual talk at the table where he normally sits for the kinds of talks we have at my table, which are generally, like, in-depth analyses of last night's episode of *Charmed* and how cute Rose McGowan's halter top was or whatever.

But Michael was totally a good sport about it, even though he thinks *Charmed* is facile. And I really did try to steer the conversation around to things a guy would like, such as *Buffy the Vampire Slayer* or Milla Jojovich.

Only it turned out I didn't even need to, because Michael is like one of those peppered moths we read about in Bio. You know, the ones that turned black when the tree bark they were camouflaged against got all sooty during the industrial revolution? He can totally adapt to any situation, and feel at ease. This is an amazing talent that I wish I had. Maybe if I did, I wouldn't feel so out of place at meetings of the Genovian Olive Growers' Association.

Anyway, today at the lunch table, someone brought up cloning, and everyone was talking about who would you clone if you could clone anyone, and people were saying like Albert Einstein so he could come back and tell us the meaning of life and stuff, or Jonas Salk so he could find a cure for cancer, and Mozart so he could finish his last requiem (whatever, that one was Boris's, of course), or Madame Pompadour so she could give us all tips on romance (Tina) or Jane Austen so she could write scathingly about current social mores and we could all benefit from her cutting wit (Lilly).

And then Michael said he would clone Kurt Cobain, because he was a musical genius who was taken too young. And then he asked me who I would clone, and I couldn't think of anyone, because there really isn't anyone dead that I would want to bring back, except maybe Grandpa, but how creepy would that be? And Grandmere would probably freak. So I just said Fat Louie, because I love Fat Louie and wouldn't mind having two of him around.

Only nobody looked very impressed by this except for Michael who said, 'That's nice,' which he probably only said because he is my boyfriend.

But, whatever, I could deal with that, I am totally used to being the only person I know who sits through *Empire Records* every time it comes on TBS and who thinks it is one of the best movies ever made – after *Star Wars* and *Dirty Dancing* and *Say Anything* and *Pretty Woman*, of course. Oh, and *Tremors* and *Twister*.

I am content to keep secret the fact that I must watch the Miss America Pageant every single year without fail, even though I know it is degrading to women and *not* a scholarship fund, considering no one bigger than a size ten ever gets into it.

I mean, I know these things about myself. It is just the way I am. And though I have tried to improve myself by watching award-winning movies such as *Crouching Tiger, Hidden Dragon* and *Gladiator*, I don't know, I just don't like them. Everybody dies at the end and besides, if there isn't any dancing or explosions, it is very difficult for me to pay attention.

So, OK, I accept these things about myself. They are just me. Like I am good at English and not so good at Algebra. Whatever.

But it wasn't until we got to Gifted and Talented today, after lunch, and Lilly started working on the shot list for this week's episode of her cable access show, *Lilly Tells It Like It Is*, and Boris got out his violin and started playing a concerto (sadly not in the supply closet because they still haven't put the door back on it), and Michael put on headphones and started working on a new song for his band, that I realized it:

I have no special talent. I have no gift. In fact, if it weren't for the fact that I am a princess, I would be the most ordinary person alive.

I mean, all my friends have these incredible things they can do: Lilly knows everything there is to know and isn't shy about saying it in front of a camera. Michael can not only play guitar and, like, fifty other instruments including the piano and drums, but he can also design whole computer programs. Boris has been playing his violin at sold-out Carnegie Hall concerts since he was eleven years old, or something. Tina Hakim Baba can read, like, a book a day. Shameeka knows everything there is to know about make-up and amoebas and Ling Su is an extremely talented artist.

But me?

Yeah, I can't do anything. I mean, nothing really well. Nothing better than anybody else.

I am just blah. I do not know why Michael even likes me, I am so talentless and boring. I mean, I guess it's a good thing my destiny as the monarch of a nation is sealed, because if I had to go apply for a job somewhere, I so fully wouldn't get it, because I'm not good at anything.

So here I am, sitting in Gifted and Talented, and there really is no getting around this basic fact:

I, Mia Thermopolis, am neither gifted nor talented.

WHAT AM I DOING IN HERE????? I DO NOT BELONG HERE!!!! I BELONG IN TECH. ED.!!!! OR DOMESTIC ARTS!!!!! I SHOULD BE MAK-ING A BIRDHOUSE OR A PIE!!!!

Just as I was writing this, Lilly leaned over and went, 'Oh my God, what is *wrong* with you? You look like you just ate a sock,' which is what we say whenever someone looks super depressed, because that is how Fat Louie always looks whenever he accidentally eats one of my socks and has to go to the vet to have it surgically removed.

Fortunately, Michael didn't hear her on account of having his headphones on. I would never have been able to confess in front of him what I confessed then to his sister, which is that I am a big talentless phoney.

'And they only put me in this class in the first place because I was flunking Algebra,' I told her.

And she went, 'You have a talent.'

I stared at her, my eyes wide and, I am afraid, filled with tears. 'Oh, yeah, what?' I was really scared I was going to cry. It must be PMS or something, because I was practically ready to start bawling.

But to my disappointment, all Lilly said was, 'Well, if you can't figure it out, I'm not going to tell you.' When I protested this, she went: 'Part of the journey of achieving self-actualization is that you have to reach it on your own, without help or guidance from others. Otherwise, you won't feel as keen a sense of accomplishment. But I will give you a hint: Right now, your talent is staring you in the face.'

I looked around, but I couldn't figure out what she was talking about. There was nothing staring me in the face that I could see. No one was looking at me at all. Boris was busy scraping away with his bow, and Michael was fingering his keyboard furiously (and silently), but that was about it. Everyone else was bent over their Kaplan review books or doodling or making sculptures out of Vaseline or whatever.

I still have no idea what Lilly was talking about. There is nothing I am talented at – except maybe telling a fish fork apart from a normal one.

I can't believe that all I thought I needed in order to achieve self-actualization was the love of the man to whom

I have pledged my heart. Knowing Michael loves me – or at least really likes me – just makes it all worse. Because his incredible talentedness just makes the fact that I am not good at anything even more obvious.

I wish I could go to the nurse's office and take a nap. But they won't let you do that unless you have a temperature, and I'm pretty sure all I have is jet lag.

I knew it was going to be a bad day. If I had had on my Queen Amidala underwear, I never would have realized how pathetic I am.

Tuesday, January 19th, World Civ.

Inventor	Invention	Benefits to Society	Cost to Society
Samuel B. Morse	Telegraph	Easier communication	Disrupted view (wires)
Thos. A. Edison	Electric light	Easier to turn on lights; Less expensive than candles	Society didn't trust them; weren't successful at first
	Phonograph	Music in the home w/o anyone playing instrument	Expensive; sound was bad at first
Ben Franklin	Franklin stove	Less fuel, easier cooking	More pollution
	Lightning rod	Less chance of house being struck	Ugly
Eli Whitney	Cotton gin	Less work	Less employment
A. Graham Bell	Telephone	Easier communications	Disrupted view (wires)
Elias Howe	Sewing machine	Less work	Less employment
Chris. Scholes	Typewriter	Easier work	Less employment
Henry Ford	Automobile assembly line	More cars	Pollution

I will never invent anything, either of benefit or cost to any
society, because I am a talentless reject.

Homework:

Algebra: probs at beginning of Chapter 11 (no review session, Mr G has mtgs – also, just started semester, so nothing to review yet. Also, not flunking any more!!!!!!)
English: update journal (How I Spent My Winter Break – 500 words)
Biology: Read Chapter 13
Health and Safety: Chapter 1: You and Your Environment
G & T: Figure out secret talent
French: Chapitre Dix
World Civ.: Chapter 13: Brave New World

Tuesday, January 19th, in the Limo on Way to Grandmere's for Princess Lesson

Things To Do:

1. Find Queen Amidala underwear.
2. Stop obsessing over whether or not Michael loves me vs. being in love with me. Be happy with what I have. Remember, lots of girls have no boyfriends at all. Or they have really gross ones with no front teeth like on Maury Povich.
3. Call Tina to compare notes on how the not-chasing-boys thing is working.
4. Do all homework. Do not get behind first day!!!!!
5. Wrap Michael's present.
6. Find out what Grandmere talked to Mom about last night. Oh, God, please do not let it be something weird like wanting to take me clay-pigeon shooting. I don't want to shoot any clay pigeons. Or anything else, for that matter.
7. Stop biting fingernails.
8. Buy cat litter.
9. Figure out secret talent.
10. GET SOME SLEEP!!!!!!!!! Boys don't like girls who have huge purple bags under their eyes. Not even perfect boys like Michael.

Tuesday, January 19th, *Still* in the Limo on Way to Grandmere's for Princess Lesson (presidential motorcade going by, stuck in traffic on FDR, underneath the United Nations)

Draft for English Journal:
How I Spent My Winter Break

I spent my Winter Break in Genovia, population 50,000. Genovia is a principality located on the Côte d'Azur between Italy and France. Genovia's main export is olive oil. Its main import is tourists. Recently, however, Genovia has begun suffering from considerable damage to its infrastructure due to foot traffic from the many yachts that dock in its harbour and

–

Wednesday, January 20, Homeroom

Oh, my God. I must have been even more tired than I thought yesterday. Apparently I fell asleep in the limo on the way to Grandmère's, and Lars couldn't even wake me up for my princess lesson! He says that when he tried, I swatted him away and called him a bad word in French (that is François' fault, not mine).

So he had Hans turn around and drive me back to the loft, then Lars carried me up three flights of stairs to my room (no joke, I weigh as much as about five Fat Louies) and my mom put me to bed.

I didn't wake up for dinner or anything. I slept until seven this morning! That is fifteen hours straight.

Wow. I must have been fried from all the excitement of being back home and seeing Michael, or something.

Or maybe I really did have jet lag, and that whole I-am-a-talentless-bum thing from yesterday wasn't rooted in my low self-esteem, but was due to a chemical imbalance from lack of REM sleep. You know they say that people who are sleep deprived start suffering from hallucinations after a while. There was a DJ who stayed up for eleven days straight, the longest-recorded period of time anyone has ever gone without sleep, and he started playing nothing but Crosby, Stills and Nash, and that's how they knew it was time to call the ambulance.

Except that even after fifteen hours of sleep, I still feel like a bit of a talentless bum. But at least today I don't feel like it's such a tragedy. I think sleeping for fifteen hours straight has given me some perspective. I mean, not everyone can be super-geniuses like Lilly and Michael. Just like not everyone can be a violin virtuoso like Boris. I have to be good at *something*. I just need to figure out what that something is. I asked

Mr G today at breakfast what he thinks I am good at, and he said he thinks I make some interesting fashion statements sometimes.

But that cannot have been what Lilly was referring to, as I was wearing my school uniform at the time she mentioned my mystery talent, which hardly leaves room for creative expression.

Mr G's remark reminded me that I still haven't found my Queen Amidala underwear. But I wasn't about to ask my stepfather if he'd seen them. EW! I try not to look at Mr Gianini's underwear when it comes back all folded from the laundry-by-the-pound place, and thankfully he extends the same courtesy to me.

And I couldn't ask my mom because once again she was dead to the world this morning. I guess pregnant women need as much sleep as teenagers and DJs.

But I had seriously better find them before Friday, or my first date with Michael will be a full-on disaster, I just know it. Like he'll probably open his present and be all, 'Uh . . . I guess it's the thought that counts.'

I probably should have just followed Mrs Hakim Baba's rules and got him a sweater.

But Michael is so not the sweater type! I realized it as we pulled up in front of his building today. He was standing there, looking all tall and manly and Heath Ledger-like . . . except for having dark hair, not blond.

And his scarf was kind of blowing in the wind, and I could see that part of his throat, you know, right beneath his Adam's apple and right above where his shirt collar opens, the part that Lars once told me if you hit someone hard enough, it would paralyse them. Michael's throat was so nice-looking, so pink and concave, that all I could think about was Mr Rochester standing out on the moor, brooding about his great love for Jane . . .

And I knew, I just knew, I was right not to have gotten him a sweater. I mean, Jane would never have given Mr Rochester a *sweater*. Ew.

Anyway, then Michael saw me and smiled and he didn't look like Mr Rochester any more, because Mr Rochester never smiled, he just looked like Michael.

And my heart turned over in my chest like it always does when I see him.

'Are you OK?' he wanted to know, as soon as he got into the limo. His eyes, so brown they are almost black – like the peat bogs Mr Rochester was always striding past out there on the moor, because if you step into a peat bog, you can sink in up to your head and never be heard of again . . . which in a way is like what happens every time I look into Michael's eyes: I fall and fall and am pretty sure I will never be able to get out of them again, but that's OK, because I love being there – looked deeply into mine. My eyes are merely grey, the colour of a New York City sidewalk.

'I called you last night,' Michael said, as his sister pushed him to move over on the seat so that she could get into the limo, too. 'But your mom said you'd passed out . . .'

'I was really, really tired,' I said, delighted by the fact that he appeared to have been worried about me. 'I slept for fifteen hours straight.'

'Whatever,' Lilly said. She was clearly not interested in the details of my sleep cycle. 'I heard from the producers of your movie.'

I was surprised. 'Really? What did they say?'

'They asked me to take a breakfast meeting with them,' Lilly said, sounding like she was trying not to brag. Only she wasn't succeeding terribly well. You could totally hear the gloating in her voice. 'Friday morning. So I won't be needing a ride.'

'Wow,' I said. 'A breakfast meeting? Really? Will they serve bagels?'

'Probably,' Lilly said.

I was impressed. I have never been invited to a breakfast meeting with producers before. Just with the Prince of Wales.

I asked Lilly if she had come up with a list of demands for the producers, and she said she had, but she wouldn't tell me what they were.

I think I am going to have to watch this movie and see what's making her so mad. My mom has it on tape. She said it was one of the funniest things she has ever seen.

But then, my mom laughs all through *Dirty Dancing*, even the parts that aren't supposed to be funny, so I don't know if she is the best judge.

Uh-oh. One of the cheerleaders (sadly, not Lana) tore her Achilles tendon doing pilates over the break, so they just announced they are holding tryouts for a replacement. The team's substitute got transferred to an all girls' school in Northampton due to having too wild a party while her parents were in Martinique.

I sincerely hope Lilly is too busy protesting about the movie of my life to protest about the new cheerleading tryouts. Last semester she made me walk around with a big sign that said *Cheerleading is sexist and not a sport*, which I am not even sure is technically true, since they have cheerleading championships on the sports channel. But it is a fact that there are no cheerleaders for the female sports in our school. Like Lana and her gang never turn out for the girls' basketball team or the girls' volleyball team, but they never miss a boys' game. So maybe the sexist part is true.

Oh, God, a geek just came in with a hall pass. A hall pass for me! I am being summoned to the office! And I didn't even do anything! Well, this time, anyway.

This is so unfair.

Wednesday, January 20, Outside Principal Gupta's Office

I can't believe it is only the second day of second semester, and already I am sitting here outside the principal's office. And I didn't even do anything! I mean, yeah, I didn't finish my homework, but I fully have a note from my stepdad. I turned it in to the administrative office first thing. It says:

Please excuse Mia for not completing her homework for Tuesday, January 19th. She was crippled with jet lag and unable to attend to her academic responsibilities last evening. She will, of course, make up the work tonight — Frank Gianini

It kind of sucks when your stepdad is also your teacher.

But why would Principal Gupta object to this? I mean, I realize it is only the second day of second semester, and already I've fallen behind. But I'm not THAT far behind.

And I haven't even seen Lana today, so it's not like I could have done anything to her or her personal belongings.

OH, MY GOD. It just occurred to me. What if they realize they made a mistake, putting me back in Gifted and Talented? I mean, because I have no gifts or talents? What if I was only put in there in the first place because of some computer glitch, and now they've corrected it, and they're going to put me in Tech. Ed. or Domestic Arts, where I belong? Oh, my God, I will have to make a spice rack!!! Or worse, a western omelette!!!

And I will never see Michael any more! OK, I will see him on the way to school and during lunch and after school and on weekends and holidays, but that's it. By taking me out of Gifted and Talented class, they will be depriving me of five whole hours of Michael a week! And true, during class we don't talk all that much, because Michael really *is* gifted and talented, unlike me, and needs to use that class period to hone his musical abilities. But still, at least we are *together*.

Oh, God, this is awful! WHY didn't Lilly just tell me what my talent is? Then I could throw it in Principal Gupta's face when she tries to deport me back to Tech. Ed.

Wait . . . who does that voice belong to? The one coming from Principal Gupta's office? It sounds kind of familiar. It sounds kind of like . . .

Wednesday, January 20, Grandmere's Limo

I cannot believe Grandmere just did this. I mean, what kind of person DOES this? Just yanks a teenager out of school?

She is supposed to be the adult. She is supposed to be setting a good example for me. And what does she do instead?

Well, first she tells a big fat LIE, and THEN she removes me from school property under false pretences.

I am telling you, if my mom or dad finds out about this, Clarisse Renaldo will be a dead woman.

She practically gave me a heart attack, you know. Good thing my cholesterol and everything is so low thanks to my vegetarian diet, otherwise I might have suffered a serious cardiac infarction, she scared me so bad, coming out of Principal Gupta's office like that and being all, 'Well, yes, we are of course praying for his quick recovery, but you know how these things can be . . .'

I felt all the blood run out of my face at the sight of her. Not just because, you know, it was Grandmere, talking to Principal Gupta, of all people, but because of what she was saying.

I stood up fast, my heart pounding so hard I thought it might go flying right out of my chest.

'What is it?' I asked, all panicky. 'Is it my dad? Is the cancer back? Is that it? You can tell me, I can take it.'

Because the reason that I, a technically illegitimate teenager (seeing as how my mom never married my dad), am heir to the throne of Genovia is that my dad can't have any more kids, on account of having been rendered sterile due to cancer. I was sure, from the way Grandmere was talking to Principal Gupta, that the cancer was back, and that my dad was going to have to go through chemo all over again . . .

'I will tell you in the car,' Grandmere said to me, stiffly. 'Come along.'

'No, really,' I said, trailing after her, with Lars trailing after me. 'You can tell me now. I can take it, I swear I can. Is Dad all right?'

'Don't worry about your homework, Mia,' Principal Gupta called to us, as we left her office. 'You just concentrate on being there for your father.'

So it was true! Dad *was* sick!

'Is it the cancer again?' I asked Grandmere as we left the school and headed down to her limo, which was parked out front by the stone lion that guards the steps up to Albert Einstein High. 'Do the doctors think it's treatable? Does he need a bone-marrow transplant? Because, you know, we're probably a match, on account of my having his hair. At least, what his hair must have looked like, back when he had some.'

It wasn't until we were safely inside the limo that Grandmere gave me a very disgusted look and said, 'Really, Amelia. There is nothing wrong with your father. There is, however, something wrong with that school of yours. Imagine, not allowing their pupils any sort of absences except in the case of illness. Ridiculous! Sometimes, you know, people need a day. A personal day, I think they call it. Well, today, Amelia, is your personal day.'

I blinked at her from my side of the limo. I couldn't quite believe what I was hearing.

'Wait a minute,' I said. 'You mean . . . Dad isn't sick?'

'*Pfuit!*' Grandmere said, her drawn-on eyebrows raised way up. 'He certainly seemed healthy enough when I spoke to him this morning.'

'Then what . . . ?' I stared at her. 'Why did you tell Principal Gupta . . . ?'

'Because otherwise she would not have allowed you out of class,' Grandmere said, glancing at her gold and diamond watch. 'And we are late, as it is. Really, there is nothing worse than an overzealous educator. They think they are helping, when in reality, you know, there are many different varieties of learning. Not all of it takes place in a classroom.'

Comprehension was beginning to dawn. Grandmere had not pulled me out of school in the middle of the day because anyone in my family was sick. No, Grandmere had pulled me out of school because she wanted to teach me something.

'Grandmere,' I cried, hardly able to believe what I was hearing. 'You can't just drive over and yank me out of school whenever you want to. And you certainly can't tell Principal Gupta that my dad is sick when he isn't! How could you even *say* something like that? Don't you know anything about karma? I mean, if you go around lying about stuff like that all the time, it could actually come true.'

'Don't be ridiculous, Amelia,' Grandmere said. 'Your father is not going to have to go back to hospital just because I told a little white lie to an academic administrator.'

'I don't know how you can be so sure of that,' I said, angrily. 'And anyway, where do you think you're taking me? I can't afford to just be leaving school in the middle of the day, you know, Grandmere. I mean, I've got a lot of catching up to do thanks to the fact that I went to bed so early last night . . .'

'Oh, I am sorry,' Grandmere said, very sarcastically. 'I know how much you enjoy your Algebra class. I am sure it is a very great deprivation to you, missing it today . . .'

I couldn't deny that she was right. At least partially. While I wasn't all that thrilled about the method by which she'd done it, the fact that Grandmere had extracted me from

109

Algebra wasn't exactly something I was about to cry over. I mean, come on. Integers are not my best thing.

'Well, wherever we're going,' I said, severely, 'we better be back in time for lunch. Because Michael will wonder where I am.'

'Not *that boy* again,' Grandmere said, lifting her gaze to the limo's sun roof with a sigh.

'Yes, *that boy*,' I said. 'That boy I happen to love with all of my heart and soul . . .'

'Oh, we're here,' Grandmere said, with some relief, as her driver pulled over. 'At last. Get out, Amelia.'

I got out of the limo, then looked around to see where Grandmere had brought me. But all I saw was the big Chanel store on Fifty-Seventh Street. That couldn't be where we were headed. Could it?

But when Grandmere, untangling Rommel from his Louis Vuitton leash, put him on the ground and then began striding purposefully towards those big glass doors, I saw that Chanel was exactly where we were headed.

'Grandmere,' I cried, rushing after her. 'Chanel? You pulled me out of class to take me *shopping*?'

'You need a gown,' Grandmere said with a sniff, 'for the black-and-white ball at the Contessa Trevanni's this Friday. This was the soonest I could get an appointment.'

'Black-and-white ball?' I echoed, as Lars escorted us into the hushed white interior of Chanel, the world's most exclusive fashion boutique – the kind of store that, before I found out I was a princess, I would have been too terrified ever even to set foot in . . . although I can't say the same for my friends, as Lilly had once filmed an entire episode of her cable access show from inside a dressing room at Chanel. She'd barricaded herself in and was trying on Karl Lagerfeld's latest creations, refusing to come out until security broke the door down and escorted her to the sidewalk. It had been a show on how haute couture designers are, judging by the way their clothes fit, really sadistic misogynists at heart. 'What black-and-white ball?'

'Surely your mother told you,' Grandmere said, as a tall, reed-thin woman approached us with cries of, 'Your Royal Highnesses! How delightful to see you.'

'My mother didn't tell me anything about a ball,' I said. 'When did you say it was?'

'Friday night,' Grandmere said to me. To the saleslady she said, 'Yes, I believe you've put aside some gowns for my granddaughter. I specifically requested white ones.' Grandmere blinked owlishly at me. 'You are too young for black. I don't want to hear any arguing about it.'

Argue about it? How could I argue about something I hadn't even begun to understand?

'Of course,' the saleslady was saying, with a big smile. 'Come with me, won't you, Your Highnesses?'

'Friday night?' I cried, that part, at least, of what was going on beginning to sink in. 'Friday night? Grandmere, I can't go to any ball on Friday night. I already made plans with—'

But Grandmere just put her hand in the centre of my back and pushed.

And then I was tripping after the saleslady, who didn't even blink an eye, as if princesses in combat boots go tripping after her all the time.

And now I am sitting in Grandmere's limo on my way back to school, and all I can think about is the number of people I would like to thank for my current predicament, foremost among which is my mother, for forgetting to tell me that she already gave Grandmere permission to drag me to this thing; the Contessa Trevanni, for having a black-and-white ball in the first place; the salespeople at Chanel, who, although they are very nice, are really all just a bunch of enablers, as they have enabled my grandma to garb me in a white, diamanté ball gown and drag me to something I have no desire to attend in the first place; my father, for setting his mother loose upon the hapless city of Manhattan without anyone to supervise her; and of course Grandmere herself, for completely ruining my life.

Because when I told her, as the Chanel people were throwing yards of fabric over me, that I cannot possibly attend Contessa Trevanni's black-and-white ball this Friday night, as that is the night Michael and I are supposed to have our first date, she responded by giving me a big lecture about how a princess's first duty is to her people. Her heart, Grandmere says, must always come second.

I tried to explain how this date could not be postponed or rescheduled, as *Star Wars* would only be showing at the Screen Room that night, and that after that they would go back to showing *Moulin Rouge*, which I can't see because I heard someone dies at the end.

But Grandmere refused to see that my date with Michael was anywhere near as important as Contessa Trevanni's black-and-white ball. Apparently Contessa Trevanni is a very socially prominent member of the Monaco royal family, besides being some kind of distant cousin (who isn't?) of ours. My not attending her black-and-white ball here in the city with all the other debutantes would be a slight from which the royal house of Renaldo might never recover.

I pointed out that my not attending *Star Wars* with Michael will be a slight from which my relationship with my boyfriend might never recover. But Grandmere said only that if Michael really loves me, he'll understand when I have to cancel.

'And if he doesn't,' Grandmere said, exhaling a plume of grey smoke from the Gitanes she was sucking down, 'then he was never appropriate consort material to begin with.'

Which is very easy for Grandmere to say. *She* hasn't been in love with Michael since the first grade. *She* doesn't spend hours and hours attempting to write poems befitting his greatness. *She* doesn't know what it is to love, since the only person Grandmere has ever been in love with in her entire life is herself.

Well, it's true.

And now we are pulling up to the school. It is lunchtime. In a minute I will have to go inside and explain to Michael how I cannot make it to our first date, or it will cause an international incident from which the country over which I will one day rule may never recover.

Why couldn't Grandmere just have shot me instead?

Wednesday, January 20, Gifted and Talented

I couldn't tell him.

I mean, how could I? Especially when he was being so nice to me during lunch. Everybody in the whole school, it seemed, knew that Grandmere had come and taken me away during second period. In her chinchilla cape, with those eyebrows, and Rommel at her side, how could anyone have missed her? She is as conspicuous as Cher.

Everyone was all concerned, you know, about the supposed illness in my family. Michael especially. He was all, 'Is there anything I can help with? Your Algebra homework, or something? I know it isn't much, but it's the least I can do . . .'

How could I tell him the truth – that my father wasn't sick; that my grandmother had dragged me off in the middle of school to take me *shopping*? Shopping for a dress to wear at a ball to which he was not invited, and which was to take place during the exact time we were supposed to have been enjoying dinner and a space fantasy set in a galaxy far far away?

I couldn't. I couldn't tell him. I couldn't tell anyone. I just sat there at lunch being all quiet. People mistook my lack of talkativeness for extreme mental duress. Which it was, actually, only not for the reasons they thought. Basically all I was thinking as I sat there was I HATE MY GRAND-MOTHER. I HATE MY GRANDMOTHER. I HATE MY GRANDMOTHER. I HATE MY GRANDMOTHER.

I really, really do.

As soon as lunch was over, I sneaked off to one of the pay phones outside the auditorium doors and called home. I knew my mom would be there instead of at her studio because she is still working on the nursery walls. She'd gotten to the third wall, on which she was depicting a highly realistic painting of the fall of Saigon.

'Oh, God, Mia,' she said, when I asked her if there wasn't something she'd possibly forgotten to mention to me. 'I am so sorry. Your grandmother called during *Ab Fab*. You know how I get during *Ab Fab*.'

'Mom,' I said, through gritted teeth. 'Why did you tell her it was OK for me to go to this stupid thing? You told me I could go out with Michael that night!'

'I did?' My mom sounded bewildered. And why shouldn't she? She clearly did not remember the conversation she'd had with me about my date with Michael . . . primarily of course because she'd been dead to the world during it. Still, she didn't need to know that. What was important was that she was made to feel as guilty as possible for the heinous crime she had committed. 'Oh, honey. I am so sorry. Well, you're just going to have to cancel Michael. He'll understand.'

'Mom,' I cried. 'He will not! This was supposed to be our first date! You've got to do something!'

'Well,' my mom said, sounding kind of wry. 'I'm a little surprised to hear you're so unhappy about it, sweetheart. You know, considering your whole thing about not wanting to chase Michael. Cancelling your first date with him would definitely fall under that category.'

'Very funny, Mom,' I said. 'But Jane wouldn't cancel her first date with Mr Rochester. She just wouldn't call him all the time beforehand, or let him get to second base during it.'

'Oh,' my mom said.

'Look,' I said. 'This is serious. You've got to get me out of this stupid ball!'

But all my mom said was that she'd talk to my dad about

it. I knew what that meant, of course. No way was I getting out of this ball. My dad has never in his life forsaken duty for love.

So now I am sitting here (doing nothing, as usual, because I am neither gifted nor talented), knowing that at some point or another I am going to have to tell Michael our date is cancelled. Only how? How am I going to do it? And what if he's so mad he never asks me out again?

Worse, what if he asks some other girl to see *Star Wars* with him? I mean, some girl who knows all the lines you're suppose to shout at the screen during the movie. Like when Ben Kenobi goes, 'Obi Wan. Now that's a name I haven't heard in a long time,' you're supposed to shout, 'How long?' and then Ben goes, 'A very long time.'

There must be a million girls besides me who know about this. Michael could ask any one of them instead of me and have a perfectly wonderful time. Without me.

Lilly is bugging to find out what's wrong. She keeps passing me notes, because they are fumigating the teachers' lounge, so Mrs Hill is in here today, pretending to grade papers from her fourth period computer class. But really she is ordering things from a Garnet Hill catalogue. I saw it beneath her gradebook.

Is your dad super-sick? Lilly's latest note reads. *Are you going to have to fly back to Genovia?*

No, I wrote back.

Is it the cancer? Lilly wants to know. *Did he have a recurrence?*

No, I wrote back.

Well, what is it, then? Lilly's handwriting was getting spiky, a sure sign she was becoming impatient with me. *Why won't you tell me?*

Because, I wanted to scrawl back, in big capital letters, *the truth will lead to the imminent demise of my romantic relationship with*

116

your brother, and I couldn't bear that! Don't you see I can't live without him?

But I couldn't write that. Because I wasn't ready to give up yet. I mean, wasn't I a princess of the royal house of Renaldo? Do princesses of the royal house of Renaldo give up, just like that, when something they hold as dearly as I hold Michael is at stake?

No, they do not. Look at my ancestresses, Agnes and Rosagunde. Agnes jumped off a bridge in order to get what she wanted (not to be a nun). And Rosagunde strangled a guy with her own hair (in order not to have to sleep with him). Was I, Mia Thermopolis, going to let a little thing like the Contessa Trevanni's black-and-white ball get in the way of my having my first date with the man I love?

No, I was not.

Perhaps this, then, is my talent. The indomitability that I inherited from the Renaldo princesses before me.

Struck by this realization, I wrote a hasty note to Lilly:

Is my talent that I, like my ancestresses before me, am indomitable?

I waited breathlessly for her response. Although it was not clear to me what I was going to do if she replied in the positive. Because what kind of talent is being indomitable? I mean, you can't get paid for it, the way you can if your talent is playing the violin or songwriting or producing cable access television programmes.

Still, it would be good to know I'd figured out my talent on my own. You know, as far as climbing the Jungian tree to self-actualization went.

But Lilly's response was way disappointing:

No, your talent is not that you're indomitable, dinkus. God, U R so dense sometimes. WHAT IS WRONG WITH YOUR DAD?????

Sighing, I realized I had no choice but to write back,

117

Nothing. Grandmere just wanted to take me to Chanel, so she made up the thing about my dad being sick.

God, Lilly wrote back. *No wonder you're looking like you ate a sock again. Your grandmother sucks.*

I could not agree more. If only Lilly knew the full extent of just how much.

Wednesday, January 20, Sixth Period, Third-floor Stairwell

Emergency meeting of the followers of the Jane Eyre technique of boyfriend-handling. We are, of course, in peril of discovery at any moment as we are skipping French in order to gather here in the stairwell leading to the roof (the door to which is locked: Lilly says in the movie of my life, the kids got to go on the roof of their school all the time. Just another example of how art most certainly does not imitate life), so that we can lend succour to one of our sisters in suffering.

That's right. It turns out that I am not the only one for whom the semester is off to an inauspicious beginning. Not only did Tina sprain her ankle on the ski slopes of Aspen – no, she also got a text message from Dave Farouq El-Abar on her new mobile phone in fifth period. It said, U NEVER CALLED BACK. AM TAKING JASMINE TO RANGERS GAME. HAVE A NICE LIFE ;-)

I have never in my life seen anything so insensitive as that text message. I swear, my blood went cold as I read it.

'Sexist pig,' Lilly said, when she saw it. 'Don't even worry about it, Tina. You'll find somebody better.'

'I d-don't want someone b-better,' Tina sobbed. 'I only want D-Dave!'

It breaks my heart to see her in such pain – not just her emotional pain, either, because it was no joke trying to get up the third-floor staircase on her crutches. I have promised faithfully to sit with her while she works through her anguish (Lilly is taking her through Elisabeth Kubler-Ross's five stages of grief: Denial – I can't believe he would do this to me; Bargaining – Maybe if I tell him I'll call him faithfully every night, he'll take me back; Anger – Jasmine is a cow

119

who Frenches on the first date; Depression – I'll never love another man again; Acceptance – Well, I guess he *was* kind of selfish). Of course, being here with Tina, instead of in French class, means I am risking possible suspension, which is the penalty for skipping class here at Albert Einstein.

But what is more important? My disciplinary record or my friend?

Besides, Lars is keeping lookout at the bottom of the stairs. If Mr Kreblutz, the chief custodian, comes along Lars is going to whistle the Genovian national anthem and we'll flatten ourselves against the wall by the old gym mats (which are quite smelly, by the way, and undoubtedly a fire hazard).

Although I am deeply saddened for her, I can't help feeling that Tina's situation has taught me a valuable lesson: that the Jane Eyre technique of boyfriend-handling is not necessarily the most reliable method by which to hang on to your boyfriend. I mean, the whole reason Dave dumped Tina is because she stopped calling him.

Except that, according to Grandmere, who did manage to hang onto a husband for forty years, the quickest way to turn a guy off is to chase after him.

And certainly Lilly, who has the longest-running relationship of any of us, does not chase after Boris. Really, if anything, *he* is the one doing the chasing. But that is probably because Lilly is too busy with her various lawsuits and projects to pay much more than perfunctory attention to him.

Somewhere between the two of them – Grandmere and Lilly – must lie the truth to maintaining a successful relationship with a man. Somehow I have got to get the hang of this, because I will tell you one thing: if I ever get a message from Michael like the one Tina just got from Dave, I will fully be taking a swan dive off the Tappanzee Bridge. And I highly doubt any cute coastguard officer is going to come along and fish me out – at least, not in one piece. The Tappanzee Bridge is WAY higher than the Pont des Vierges.

Of course you know what this means – this whole thing with Tina and Dave, I mean. It means that I can't cancel my date with Michael. No way, no how. I don't care if Monaco starts lobbing SCUD missiles at the Genovian House of Parliament: I am not going to that black-and-white ball. Grandmere and the Contessa Trevanni are just going to have to learn how to live with disappointment.

Because when it comes to our men, we Renaldo women don't mess around. We play for keeps. And we have the battle scars to prove it.

Homework:

Algebra: probs at beginning of Ch 11, PLUS ??? Don't know, thanks to Grandmere
English: update journal (How I Spent My Winter Break – 500 words) PLUS ??? Don't know, thanks to Grandmere
Biology: Read Chapter 13, PLUS ??? Don't know, thanks to Grandmere
Health and Safety: Chapter 1: You and Your Environment PLUS ??? Don't know, thanks to Grandmere
G & T: Figure out secret talent
French: Chapitre Dix PLUS Don't know, due to skipping!!!!
World Civ.: Chapter 13: Brave New World; bring in current event illustrating how technology can cost society

Wednesday, January 20, Limo on the Way Home from Grandmere's

I don't believe this.

Apparently it is not enough that Grandmere has to disrupt my entire school day with her spur-of-the-moment illicit shopping trips. Oh, no. Apparently she won't be satisfied until she has destroyed my love life, too.

That's right, DESTROYED my love life.

It is clear to me now that this has been her goal all along. The simple fact of the matter is, Grandmere can't stand Michael. Not, of course, because he's ever done anything to her. Never done anything to her except make her granddaughter superbly, sublimely happy.

No, Grandmere doesn't like Michael because Michael is not royal.

How do I know this? Well, it became pretty obvious when I walked into her suite for my princess lesson today, and who should just be coming in from his tennis lesson at the New York Health and Racquet Club, swinging his racquet and looking all Andre Agassi-ish? Oh, only Prince René.

'What are YOU doing here?' I demanded, in a manner that Grandmere later reproved me for (she said my question was unladylike in its accusatory tone, as if I suspected René of something underhanded, which, of course, I did, as he has never shown any marked interest in the plight of Genovia's sea turtles and dolphins, which will soon be endangered, if we don't stop jet-setters like René from recklessly polluting their habitat).

'Enjoying your beautiful city,' was how René replied. And then he excused himself to go shower, as he was smelling a bit ripe from the court.

'Really, Amelia,' Grandmere said, disapprovingly. 'Is that any way to greet your cousin?'

'Why isn't he back in school?' I wanted to know.

'For your information,' Grandmere said, 'he happens to be on a break.'

'Still?' This sounds pretty suspicious to me. I mean, what kind of business college – even a French one – has a Christmas break that goes on practically into February?

'European schools,' was Grandmere's explanation for this, 'traditionally have a longer winter holiday than American ones, so that their pupils can make full use of the ski season.'

'I didn't see any skis on him,' I pointed out, craftily.

'*Pfuit!*' was all Grandmere had to say about it, however. 'René has never been to Manhattan. Of course I invited him along. He wants to experience the city that never sleeps.'

Well, I guess I can see that. I mean, New York *is* the greatest city in the world, after all. Why, just the other day, a construction worker down on Forty-Second Street found a twenty-pound rat! That's a rat that's only five pounds lighter than my cat! You won't be finding any twenty-pound rats in Paris or Hong Kong, that's for darn sure.

So, anyway, we were going along, doing the princess lesson thing – you know, Grandmere was instructing me about all the personages I was going to meet at this black-and-white ball, including this year's crop of debutantes, the daughters of socialites and other so-called American royalty, who were 'coming out' to Society with a capital S, and looking for husbands (even though what they should be looking for, if you ask me, is a good undergraduate programme, and maybe a part-time job teaching illiterate homeless people to read – but that's just me) when all of a sudden it occurred to me – the solution to my problem:

Why couldn't Michael be my escort to the Contessa Trevanni's black-and-white ball?

OK, granted, it was no *Star Wars*. And yeah, he'd have to get his hands on a tux and all. But at least we would be together. At least I could still give him his birthday present somewhere outside of the cinderblock walls of Albert Einstein High. At least I wouldn't have to cancel altogether. At least the state of diplomatic affairs between Genovia and Monaco would remain at DEFCON 5.

But how, I wondered, was I ever going to get Grandmere to go along with it? I mean, she hadn't said anything about the contessa letting me bring a date.

Still, what about all those debutantes? Weren't they bringing dates? Wasn't that what West Point Military Academy was *for*? Providing dates for debutante balls? And if those girls could bring dates, and they weren't even princesses, why couldn't I?

How I was going to get Grandmere to let me bring Michael to the black-and-white ball, after all of our long discussions about how you mustn't let the object of your affection even know that you like him, was going to be a major obstacle. I decided I would have to exercise some of the diplomatic tact Grandmere had taken so much trouble to teach me.

'And please, whatever else you do, Amelia,' Grandmere was saying, as she sat there running a metal comb through Rommel's sparse – and getting sparser – fur, as the royal Genovian vet had instructed, 'do not stare too long at the contessa's facelift. I know it will be difficult – it looks as if the surgeon botched it horribly. But actually, it's exactly the way Elena wanted it to look. Apparently she has always fancied resembling an anteater—'

'Listen, about this dance, Grandmere,' I started in, all

subtly. 'Do you think the contessa would mind if I, you know, brought someone?'

Grandmere looked at me confusedly over Rommel's pink, trembling body. 'What do you mean? Amelia, I highly doubt your mother would have a very nice time at the contessa Trevanni's black-and-white ball. For one thing, there won't be any other hippy radicals there . . .'

'Not my mom,' I said, realizing that perhaps I had been a little *too* subtle. 'I was thinking more, you know, of an escort.'

'But you already have an escort.' Grandmere adjusted Rommel's diamond-chip-encrusted collar.

'I do?' I did not recall asking anyone to scrounge up a West Pointer for me.

'Of course you do,' Grandmere said, still not, I noticed, meeting my gaze. 'Prince René has very generously offered to serve as your escort to the ball. Now, where were we? Oh, yes. About the contessa's taste in clothes. I think you've learned enough by now to know that you aren't to comment – at least to her face – on what your hostess happens to be wearing. But I think it necessary to warn you that the contessa has a tendency to wear clothes that are somewhat young on her, and that reveal—'

'*René* is going to be my escort?' I stood up, nearly knocking Grandmere's maid, who'd come to refresh her mistress's Sidecar, off her feet as I did so. '*René* is taking me to the black-and-white ball?'

'Well, yes,' Grandmere said, looking blandly innocent – a little too blandly innocent, if you asked me. 'He is, after all, a stranger to the city – to this country, as a matter of fact. I would think that you, Amelia, would be only too happy to make him feel welcome and wanted . . .'

I narrowed my eyes at her. 'What is going on here?' I

demanded. 'Grandmere, are you trying to fix up Prince René and me?'

'Certainly not,' Grandmere said, looking genuinely appalled by the suggestion. But then, I'd been fooled by Grandmere's expressions before. Especially the one she puts on when she wants you to think that she is just a helpless old lady. 'Your imagination most definitely comes from your mother's side of the family. Your father was never as fanciful as you are, Amelia, for which I can only thank God. He'd have driven me to an early grave, I'm convinced of it, if he'd been half as capricious as you tend to be, young lady.'

'Well, what else am I supposed to think?' I asked, feeling a little sheepish over my outburst. After all, the idea that Grandmere might, even though I am only fourteen, be trying to fix me up with some prince that she wants me to marry *is* a little outlandish. I mean, even for Grandmere. Still, if it *walks* like a duck, and *talks* like a duck . . . 'I mean, first that thing with making us dance together . . .'

'For a magazine pictorial,' Grandmere sniffed.

'. . . and then your not liking Michael . . .'

'I never said I didn't like him. I think he is a perfectly charming boy. I just want you to be realistic about the fact that you, Amelia, are not like other girls. You are a princess, and have the good of your country to think of.'

'. . . and then René showing up like this, and your announcing that he's taking me to the black-and-white ball . . .'

'Is it wrong of me to want to see the poor boy have a nice time while he is here? He has suffered so many hardships, losing his ancestral home, not to mention his own principality.'

'Grandmere,' I said. 'René's principality got absorbed into Italy, like, three hundred years ago. He wasn't even alive when it happened.'

'A man without a country,' Grandmere said, 'is like a man without a soul.'

Great. And this is my date for the Contessa Trevanni's black-and-white ball. A man without a soul. What next, I ask you? Brunch with Count Dracula?

And what am I supposed to do now? About Michael, I mean? I can't bring both him *and* Prince René to the ball. I mean, I look weird enough, with my half-grown-out hair and my androgyny (although judging by Grandmere's description of her, the contessa might look even weirder than I do) without hauling two dates and a bodyguard around with me.

This new year is not turning out to be very propitious for any of us. I mean, first Tina sprains her ankle, then loses her one true love; then I get saddled with Prince René, a black-and-white ball, and the realization that I am one hundred per cent not talented at anything . . . well, except for maybe one thing, only I don't know what it is, and the person who does know won't tell me because I am supposed to figure it out on my own.

But I can't even figure out how to explain to my boyfriend that I can't make our very first date with one another. How am I supposed to figure out what my secret talent is?????

Wednesday, January 20, the Loft

Well, my mom getting hold of my dad was a washout. Apparently the whole parking fees debate has gotten way out of control. The Minister of Tourism is conducting a filibuster, and there can't be a vote until he stops talking and sits down. So far he's been talking for twelve hours, forty-eight minutes. I don't know why my dad doesn't just have him arrested and put in the dungeon. According to my mom, that would be a violation of the minister's right to free speech. But what about my dad's right to take phone calls from the mother of his only child? Who is safeguarding that right, I would like to know?

I am really starting to be afraid that I am not going to be able to get out of this ball thingy.

'You better let Michael know,' my mom just poked her head in to say, helpfully, 'that you won't be able to make it Friday. Hey, are you writing in your journal again? Aren't you supposed to be doing your homework?'

Trying to change the subject from my homework (hello, I am totally doing it, I am just taking a break right now), I went, 'Mom, I am not saying anything to Michael until we've heard from Dad. Because there's no point in my running the risk of Michael breaking up with me if Dad's just going to turn around and say I don't have to go to the stupid ball.'

'Mia,' my mom said, 'Michael is not going to break up with you just because you have a familial commitment you cannot get out of.'

'I wouldn't be so sure,' I said, darkly. 'Dave Farouq El-Abar broke up with Tina today because she didn't return his call.'

'That's different,' my mom said. 'It's just plain rude not to return someone's calls.'

'But Mom,' I said. I was getting tired of having to explain this stuff to my mom all the time. It is a wonder to me she ever got a single guy in the first place, let alone two of them, when she clearly knows so little about the art of dating. 'If you are too available, the guy might think all the thrill has gone out of the chase.'

My mother looked suspicious. 'Don't tell me. Let me guess. Your grandmother told you that?'

'Um,' I said. 'Yes.'

'Well, let me give you a little tip my mother once gave me,' my mom said. I was surprised. My mom doesn't get along so well with her parents, Mamaw and Papaw, who run the Handy Dandy Hardware Store of Versailles, Indiana. It is rare that she mentions either of them ever giving her a piece of advice worthy of passing down to her own daughter, as my mom ran away from home as soon as she was financially able to, and has only been back there, like, twice.

'If you think there's a chance you might have to cancel on Michael for Friday night,' she said, 'you'd better cat-on-the-roof him now.'

I was understandably perplexed by this. 'Cat on the whatta?'

'Cat on the roof,' my mother said. 'You need to begin mentally preparing him for the disappointment. For instance, if something had happened to Fat Louie while you were in Genovia—' My mouth must have fallen open, since my mom went, 'Don't worry, nothing did. But I'm just saying, if something had, I would not have blurted it right out to you, over the phone. I'd have prepared you gently for the eventual letdown. Like I might have said, "Mia, Fat Louie escaped through your window and now he's up on the roof, and we can't get him down".'

'Of course you could get him down,' I protested. 'You

could go up by the fire escape and take a pillowcase and when you get near him, you could throw the pillowcase over him and scoop him up and carry him back down again.'

'Yes,' my mom said. 'But supposing I told you I'd try that. And the next day I called you and said it hadn't worked, Fat Louie had escaped to the neighbour's roof—'

'I'd tell you to go to the building next door and make someone let you in, then go up to their roof.' I really did not see where this was going. 'Mom, how could you be so irresponsible as to let Fat Louie out in the first place? I've told you again and again – you've got to keep my bedroom window closed, you know how he likes to watch the pigeons. Louie doesn't have any outdoor survival skills . . .'

'So naturally,' my mom said, 'you wouldn't expect him to survive two nights out of doors.'

'No,' I practically wailed. 'I wouldn't.'

'Right. See. So you'd be mentally prepared when I called you on the third day to say despite everything we'd done, Louie was dead.'

'OH, MY GOD!' I snatched up Fat Louie from where he was lying beside me on the bed. 'And you think I should do that to poor Michael? He has a dog, not a cat! Pavlov's never going to get up on the roof!'

'No,' my mother said, looking tired. Well, and why not? She was hauling around a dozen or so extra pounds all of a sudden. 'I'm saying you should begin mentally preparing Michael for the disappointment he is going to feel if, indeed, you need to cancel him on Friday night. Call him and tell him you might not be able to make it. That's all. Cat-on-the-roof him.'

I let Fat Louie go. Not just because I finally realized what my mom was getting at, but because he was trying to bite

130

me in order to get me to loosen the stranglehold I had on him.

'Oh,' I said. 'You think if I do that – start mentally preparing him for my not being able to go out with him on Friday – he won't dump me when I get around to breaking the actual news?'

'Mia,' my mom said. 'No boy is going to dump you because you have to cancel a date. If any boy does, then he wasn't worth going out with anyway. Much like Tina's Dave, I'd venture to say. She's probably better off without him. Now. Do your homework.'

Only how could anyone expect me to do my homework after imparting a piece of information like that?

Instead I went online. I meant to instant message Michael, but I found that Tina was instant messaging me.

```
Iluvromance: Hi, Mia. What R U doing?
```

She sounded so sad! She was even using a blue font!

```
FtLouie:  I'm just doing my Bio. How are you?
>
Iluvromance:  OK, I guess. I just miss him so
              much!!!!!!!!!!!!!!!!!!!!!!!! I wish I had
              never even heard of stupid Jane Eyre.
```

Remembering what my mom had said, I wrote:

```
FtLouie:  Tina, if Dave was willing to break up
          with you just because you didn't return
          his calls, then he was not worthy of
          you. You will find a new boy, one who
          appreciates you.
```

```
>
Iluvromance: Do U really think so?
>
FtLouie: Absolutely.
>
Iluvromance: But where am I going to find a boy who
             appreC8s me at AEHS? All the boys who go
             there are morons. Except MM of course.
>
FtLouie: Don't worry, we'll find someone for you.
         I have to go IM my dad now . . .
```

I didn't want to tell her that the person I really had to IM was Michael. I didn't want to rub it in that I had a boyfriend and she didn't. Also, I hoped she didn't remember that in Genovia, where my dad was, it was four o'clock in the morning. Also that the Palais de Genovia doesn't have instant messaging.

```
FtLouie: . . . so TTYL.
>
Iluvromance: OK, bye. If U feel like chatting
             later, I'll be here. I have nowhere else
             to go.
```

Poor, sweet Tina! She is clearly prostrate with grief. Really, if you think about it, she is well rid of Dave. If he wanted to leave her for this Jasmine girl so badly he could have let her down gently by cat-on-the-roofing her. If he were any kind of gentleman, he would have. But it was all too clear now that Dave was no gentleman at all.

I'm glad MY boyfriend is so different. Or at least, I hope he is. No, wait, of course he is. He's MICHAEL.

```
FtLouie:   Hey!
>
LinuxRulz: Hey back atcha! Where have you been?
>
FtLouie:   Princess lessons.
>
LinuxRulz: Don't you know everything there is to
           know about being a princess yet?
>
FtLouie:   Apparently not. Grandmere's got me in
           for some fine tuning. Speaking of which,
           is there, like, a later showing of Star
           Wars than the seven o'clock?
>
LinuxRulz: Yeah, there's an eleven. Why?
>
FtLouie:   Oh, nothing.
>
LinuxRulz: WHY?
```

But see, here was the part where I couldn't do it. Maybe because of the capital letters, or maybe because my conversation with Tina was still too fresh in my mind. The unparalleled sadness in her blue U letters was just too much for me. I know I should have just come right out and told him about the ball thingy then and there, only I couldn't go through with it. All I could think about was how incredibly smart and gifted Michael is, and what a pathetic, talentless freak I am, and how easy it would be for him to go out and find someone worthier of his attentions.

So instead, I wrote:

```
FtLouie:   I've been trying to think of some names
           for your band.
```

133

>

LinuxRulz: What does that have to do with whether or not there's a later showing of Star Wars Friday night?

>

FtLouie: Well, nothing, I guess. Except what do you think of Michael and the Wookies?

>

LinuxRulz: I think maybe you've been playing with Fat Louie's catnip mouse again.

>

FtLouie: Ha ha. OK, how about The Ewoks?

>

LinuxRulz: The EWOKS? Where did your grandma take you today when she hauled you out of second period? Electric shock therapy?

>

FtLouie: I'm only trying to help.

>

LinuxRulz: I know, sorry. Only I don't think the guys would really enjoy being equated with furry little muppets from the planet Endor. I mean, I know one of them is Boris, but even he would draw the line at Ewoks, I hope . . .

FtLouie: BORIS PELKOWSKI IS IN YOUR BAND????

>

LinuxRulz: Yeah. Why?

>

FtLouie: Nothing.

All I can say is, if I had a band, I would NOT let Boris in

it. I mean, I know he is a talented musician and all, but he is also a mouth breather. I think it's great that he and Lilly get along so well, and for short periods of time I can totally put up with him and even have a nice time with him and all. But I would not let him be in my band. Not unless he stopped tucking his sweaters into his pants.

```
LinuxRulz: Boris isn't so bad, once you get to know
           him.
>
FtLouie:   I know. He just doesn't seem like the
           band type. All that Bartok.
>
LinuxRulz: He plays a mean bluegrass, you know. Not
           that we'll be playing any bluegrass in
           the band.
```

This was comforting to know.

```
LinuxRulz: So will your grandmother let you off on
           time?
```

I genuinely had no idea what he was talking about.

```
FtLouie:   What????
>
LinuxRulz: On Friday. You've got princess lessons,
           right? That's why you were asking about
           later showings of the movie, wasn't it?
           You're worried your grandmother isn't
           going to let you out on time?
```

This is where I screwed up. You see, he had offered me

the perfect get-out – I could have said, 'Yes, I am,' and chances were, he'd have been like, 'OK, well, let's make it another time, then.'

BUT WHAT IF THERE WERE NO OTHER TIME????

What if Michael, like Dave, just blew me off and found some other girl to take to the show????

So instead, I went:

```
FtLouie:   No, it will be OK. I think I can get off
           early.
```

WHY AM I SO STUPID???? WHY DID I WRITE THAT???? Because of COURSE I won't be able to get off early, I will be at the stupid black-and-white ball ALL NIGHT!!!!!

I swear, I am such an idiot, I don't even deserve to have a boyfriend.

Thursday, January 21, Homeroom

This morning at breakfast, Mr G was all, 'Has anyone seen my brown corduroy pants?' and my mom, who had set her alarm so that she could wake up early enough to possibly catch my dad on a break between Parliament sessions (no such luck), went, 'No, but has anyone seen my Free Winona T-shirt?'

And then I went, 'Well, I still haven't found my Queen Amidala underwear.'

And that's when we all realized it: someone had stolen our laundry.

It is really the only explanation for it. I mean, we send laundry out, to the Thompson Street laundry-by-the-pound place, and then they do it for us and deliver it all folded and stuff. Since we don't have a doorman, generally the bag just sits in the vestibule until one of us picks it up and drags it up the three flights of stairs to the loft.

Only apparently, no one has seen the bag of laundry we dropped off the day before I left for Genovia!

Which can only mean that some freaky newsreporter (they regularly go through our garbage, much to the chagrin of Mr Molina, our building's superintendent) found our bag of laundry, and any minute we can expect a ground-breaking news story on the front cover of the *Post*: *Out of the Closet: What Princess Mia Wears, and What it Means, According to our Experts.*

AND THEN THE WHOLE WORLD WILL FIND OUT THAT I WEAR QUEEN AMIDALA PANTIES!

I mean, it is not like I go around ADVERTISING that I have *Star Wars* underwear, or even that I have any kind of lucky panties at all. And by rights, I should have taken my

Queen Amidala underwear with me to Genovia, for luck on my Christmas Eve address to my people. If I had, maybe I wouldn't have gone off on that six-pack-holder tangent.

But, whatever, I had been too caught up in the whole Michael thing, and had completely forgotten.

And now it looks like someone has gotten hold of my special lucky underwear, and the next thing you know, it will be showing up on Ebay! Seriously! There is a ton of Princess Mia stuff being sold on Ebay, like used copies of the unauthorized biographies of my life. Who is to say my underwear wouldn't sell like hotcakes? Especially the fact that they are Queen Amidala panties.

I am so, so dead.

Mom has already called the 6th Precinct to report the theft, but those guys are too busy defusing bombs and tracking down real criminals to go after a laundry swiper. They practically laughed her off the phone.

It is all very well for her and Mr G – all they lost were regular clothes. I am the only one who lost underwear. Worse, my lucky underwear. Though I fully understand that the men and women who fight crime in this city have more important things to do than look for my panties.

But the way things have been going, I really, really need all the good luck I can get.

Thursday, January 21, Algebra

Today, before class started, Lana was on her mobile, and this is what I overheard her saying:

'No, I can't make it to Pam's on Friday, I've got this stupid thing to go to. I don't know, it's some patient of my dad's. Every year she has this stupid dance where everybody has to dress up in black and white.'

I froze, my Algebra I–II textbook only halfway open. Lana's dad, I remembered, all of my blood turning cold, is a plastic surgeon. Could he have been the one who gave Contessa Trevanni her anteater face?

'I don't know,' Lana was saying, into her phone. 'She claims to be some kind of countess. I swear to God, this town is littered with wannabe royals.'

As she said the words *wannabe royals*, Lana swivelled her head around – getting her long, shiny blonde hair all over Chapter Twelve of my Algebra book – and looked at me.

Um, excuse me. I *never* wanted to be royal. Never, ever, ever did I even remotely suggest to anyone that I thought it might be cool to be a princess.

Oh, sure, I wouldn't mind being a princess the way Belle became a princess at the end of *Beauty and the Beast*. You know, a fairy-tale princess with no problems or responsibilities, except to look pretty and be all sweet to people.

But being a princess in real life is nothing like that. You have to make all these decisions that affect the good of your country. Like should you or should you not make tourists pay for parking? And should you, or should you not, protect dolphins and sea turtles from pollution?

Clearly Lana has never thought about any of this, however.

'No, I'm not taking Josh,' she said scornfully into the

phone, as more of her stupid hair fell all over my textbook. In fact, I thought about closing my book on her hair, just to hear her scream, but I wanted to hear why she wasn't taking her long-time boyfriend, Josh Richter, to the black-and-white ball with her.

'He is so immature at these things,' Lana said to her friend. 'I mean, at the last one we went to together, he actually started throwing grapes down the front of this one girl's dress. I know. High-school boys just don't know how to act. Besides, there'll be all these West Pointers there. It'll be nice to be with some *college* boys for a change.'

Really, I may not have had a boyfriend all that long (thirty-four days to be exact) but it seems pretty disloyal to be looking forward to going to a dance with someone other than your significant other. I mean, I am totally dreading going to the contessa's black-and-white ball without Michael.

And now I am dreading it even more, knowing that Lana is going to be there.

Especially when Mr G walked into the classroom, and Lana – who had learned a lesson from last time – went, 'Oops, gotta go,' into her mobile and hung up, then happened to glance in my direction.

'What are *you* looking at, fish breath?' she wanted to know.

Now, I happen to know that I don't have fish breath. For one thing, I fully had oatmeal for breakfast, and for another, Lars is addicted to those Listerine Pocket Pak thingies that melt on your tongue and is always handing them out, and I had just had one in anticipation of Michael possibly stopping by my Algebra class on his way to Senior English (which he did, to hand me a CD he burned for me last night of Pearl Jam's greatest hits, even though of course I don't really like bands that don't have girls in them, except

*NSYNC of course, but I will totally pretend that I listened to it and liked it).

So I know that my breath did not smell like fish.

But I didn't get to say anything back to Lana because Mr G told us to get out last night's homework problems (which I actually had done) so my opportunity was cut off.

But I am going to remember what she said for ever, because we Renaldo women, we can really hold a grudge when we want to.

<u>Defn</u>: Square root of perfect sq. is either of the identical factors
<u>Defn</u>: Positive sq. root is called the principal sq. root
Negative numbers have no sq. root

Things to Do:

1. Have Genovian ambassador to the UN call the CIA. See if they can dispatch some agents to track down my underwear (if it falls into the wrong hands, could be an international incident!)
2. Get cat food!!!!!
3. Check on Mom's folic-acid intake.
4. Tell Michael I will not be able to make first date with him.
5. Prepare to be dumped.

Thursday, January 21, Health and Safety

Did you see that? They are meeting at Cosi for lunch!

Yes. He so loves her.

It's so cute when teachers are in love.

So are you nervous about your breakfast meeting tomorrow?

Hardly. THEY are the ones who should be nervous.

Are you going all by yourself? Your mom and dad aren't coming with you, are they?

Please. I can handle a bunch of movie executives on my own, thanks. God, how can they keep stuffing this infantile swill down our throats, year after year. Don't they think we know by now that tobacco kills? Hey, did you get all your homework done, or were you up all night instant messaging my brother instead?

Both.

You two are so cute, it makes me want to puke. Almost as cute as Mr Wheeton and Mademoiselle Klein.

Shut up.

God, this is boring. Want to make another list?

OK, you start.

Lilly Moscovitz's Guide to What's Hot and What's Not on TV

(with commentary by Mia Thermopolis):

Seventh Heaven

Lilly: *A complex look at one family's struggles to maintain Christian mores in an ever-evolving, modern-day society. Fairly well acted and occasionally moving, this show can turn 'preachy', but does depict the problems facing normal families with surprising realism, and only occasionally sinks to the banal.*

Mia: Even though the dad is a minister and everyone has to learn a lesson at the end of every episode, this show is pretty good. High point: When the Olsen twins guest-starred. Low point: When the show's cosmetician gave the youngest girl straight hair.

Popstars

Lilly: *A ridiculous attempt to pander to the lowest common denominator, this show puts its young stars through a humiliatingly public 'audition', then zeroes in as the losers cry and winners gloat.*

Mia: They take a bunch of attractive people who can sing and dance and make them audition for a place in a pop group, and some of them get it and some of them don't, and the ones who do are instant celebrities who then crack up, all the while wearing interesting and generally navel-baring outfits. How could this show be bad?

Sabrina the Teenage Witch

Lilly: *Though based on comic-book characters, this show is surprisingly affable, and even occasionally amusing. Although, sadly, actual Wiccan practices are not described. The show could benefit from* some research into the age-old religion that has, through the centuries, empowered millions, primarily females. The talking cat is a bit suspect: I have not read any believable documentation that would support the possibility of transfiguration.

Mia: Totally awesome during the high school/Harvey years. Goodbye Harvey = goodbye show.

Baywatch

Lilly: Puerile garbage.

Mia: Most excellent show of all time. Everyone is good-looking; you can fully follow every plotline, even while instant messaging; and there are lots of pictures of the beach, which is great when you are in dark gloomy Manhattan in February. Best episode: when Pamela Anderson Lee got kidnapped by that half-man/half-beast, who after plastic surgery became a professor at UCLA. Worst episode: anytime Mitch adopts a son.

Powerpuff Girls

Lilly: Best show on television.

Mia: Ditto. Nuff said.

Roswell High

Lilly: An intriguing look at the possibility that aliens live among us. The fact that they might be teenagers, and extraordinarily attractive ones at that, stretches the show's credibility somewhat.

Mia: Hot guys with alien powers. What more can you ask? High point: Future Max; any time anybody made out in the eraser room. Low point: when that skanky Tess showed up.

Buffy the Vampire Slayer

Lilly: *Feminist empowerment at its peak, entertainment at its best. The heroine is a lean, mean, vampire-killing machine, who worries as much about her immortal soul as she does messing up her hair. A strong role model for young women — nay, people of all sexes and ages will benefit from the viewing of this show. All of television should be this good. The fact that this show has, for so long, been ignored by the Emmys is a travesty.*

Mia: If only the Buffster could just find a boyfriend who doesn't need to drink platelets to survive. High point: any time there's kissing. Low point: none.

Gilmore Girls

Lilly: *Thoughtful portrayal of single mother struggling to raise teenage daughter in a small, northeastern town.*

Mia: Many, many, many, many, many, many cute boys. Plus it is nice to see single moms who sleep with their kid's teacher getting respect instead of lectures from the Moral Majority.

Charmed

Lilly: *While this show at least accurately portrays historical Wiccan practices, the spells these girls routinely cast are completely unrealistic. You cannot, for instance, travel through time or between dimensions without creating rifts in the space-time continuum. Were these girls really to transport themselves to seventeenth-century Puritan America, they would arrive there with their oesophaguses ripped inside out, not neatly stuffed into a corset, as no one can travel through a wormhole and maintain their mass integrity. It is a simple matter of physics. Albert Einstein must be spinning in his grave.*

146

Mia: Hello, witches in hot clothes. Like Sabrina, only better because the boys are cuter, and sometimes they are in danger and the girls have to save them.

Thursday, January 21, Gifted and Talented

Tina is so mad at Jane Eyre. She says Jane Eyre ruined her life.

She announced this at lunch. Right in front of Michael, who isn't supposed to know about the whole Jane Eyre technique of not chasing boys thing, but, whatever. He admitted to never having read the book, so I think it is a safe bet he didn't know what Tina was talking about.

Still, it was way sad. Tina said she is giving up her romance novels. Giving them up because they led to the ruination of her relationship with Dave!

We were all very upset to hear about this. Tina *loves* reading romances. She reads about one a day.

But now she says that if it weren't for romance novels, she, and not this mysterious Jasmine person, would be going to the Rangers game with Dave Farouq El-Abar this Saturday.

And my pointing out that she doesn't even like hockey didn't seem to help.

Lilly and I both realized that this was a pivotal moment in Tina's adolescent growth. It needed to be pointed out to her that Dave, not Jane, was the one who'd pulled the plug on their relationship . . . and, that when looked at objectively, the whole thing was probably for the best. It was ludicrous for Tina to blame romance novels for her plight.

So Lilly and I very quickly drew up the following list, and presented it to Tina, in the hope that she would see the error of her ways:

Mia and Lilly's List of Romantic Heroines and the Valuable Lessons Each Taught Us:

1. **Jane Eyre from *Jane Eyre*:**
   Stick to your convictions and you will prevail.
2. **Lorna Doone from *Lorna Doone*:**
   Probably you are secretly royalty and an heiress, only no one has told you yet (this applies to Mia Thermopolis, as well).
3. **Elizabeth Bennet from *Pride and Prejudice*:**
   Boys like it when you are smart-alecky.
4. **Scarlett O'Hara from *Gone with the Wind*:**
   Ditto.
5. **Maid Marian from *Robin Hood*:**
   It is a good idea to learn how to use a bow and arrow.
6. **Jo March from *Little Women*:**
   Always keep a second copy of your manuscript handy in case your vindictive little sister throws your first draft on the fire.
7. **Anne Shirley from *Anne of Green Gables*:**
   One word: Clairol.
8. **Marguerite St Juste from *The Scarlet Pimpernel*:**
   Check out your husband's rings before you marry him.
9. **Cathy, from *Wuthering Heights*:**
   Don't get too big for your breeches or you too will have to wander the moors in lonely heartbreak after you die.
10. **Juliet from *Romeo and Juliet*:**
    If you're going to fake your own death, it might be nice if you clued your husband in about it first, to avoid any tragic mishaps later.

Tina, after reading the list, admitted tearfully that we were right, that romantic heroines really were her friends, and that she could not, in good conscience, forsake them. We were all just breathing a sigh of relief (except for Michael and Boris; they were playing on Michael's Gameboy) when Shameeka made a sudden announcement, even more startling than Tina's:

'I'm trying out for cheerleading.'

We were, of course, stunned. Not because Shameeka would make a bad cheerleader – she is the most athletic of us all, also the most attractive, and knows almost as much as Tina does about fashion and make-up.

It was just that, as Lilly so bluntly put it, 'Why would you want to go and do something like *that*?'

'Because,' Shameeka explained, 'I am tired of letting Lana and her friends push me around. I am just as good as any of them. Why shouldn't I try out for the squad, even if I'm not in their little clique? I have just as good a chance of getting on the team as anybody else.'

Lilly said, 'While this is unarguably true, I feel I must warn you, Shameeka, if you try out for cheerleading, you might actually get on the squad. Are you prepared to subject yourself to the humiliation of cheering for Josh Richter as he chases after a little ball?'

'Cheerleading has, for many years, suffered from the stigma of being inherently sexist,' Shameeka said. 'But I think the cheerleading community in general is making strides at asserting itself as a fast-growing sport for both men and women. It is a good way to keep fit and active, it combines two things I love dearly, dance and gymnastics, and will look excellent on my college applications. That is, of course, the only reason my father is allowing me to try out.

150

That and the fact that I won't be allowed to attend any post-game parties.'

I didn't doubt this last part. Mr Taylor, Shameeka's dad, is way strict.

But as for the rest of it, well, I wasn't sure.

'Does that mean that if you get on the squad,' I wanted to know, 'you'll stop eating lunch with us and go sit over there?'

I pointed at the long table across the cafeteria from ours, at which Lana and Josh and all of their school-spirit minded, incredibly well-coiffed cronies sat. The thought of losing Shameeka, who was always so elegant and yet at the same time sensible, to the Dark Side made my heart ache.

'Of course not,' Shameeka said, disparagingly. 'Getting on to the Albert Einstein High School cheerleading squad is not going to change my friendships with all of you one iota. I will still be the camera person for your television show . . .' she nodded to Lilly, '. . . and your Bio. partner . . .' to me, '. . . and your lipstick consultant . . .' to Tina, '. . . and your portrait model,' to Ling Su. 'I just may not be around as much, if I get on to the squad.'

We all sat there, reflecting upon this great change that might befall us. If Shameeka made the squad it would, of course, strike a blow for geeky girls everywhere. But it would also necessarily rob of us Shameeka, who would be forced to spend all of her free time practising doing the splits and taking the bus to Mount Kisco for away games with Phillips Prep.

The silence at the table was palpable . . . well, except for the *bing-bing-bing* of Michael's electronic game. Boys – apparently even perfect boys, like Michael – are immune to things like mood.

But I can tell you, the mood of this year so far has been

pretty bad. In fact, if things don't start looking up soon, I may have to write this entire year off as a do-over.

Still no clue as to what my secret talent might be. One thing I'm pretty sure it's not is psychology. It was hard work talking Tina out of giving up her books! And we didn't manage to convince Shameeka not to try out for cheerleading. I guess I can see why she'd want to do it – I mean, it might be a *little* fun.

Though why anyone would willingly want to spend that much time with Lana Weinberger is beyond me.

Thursday, January 21, French

Mademoiselle Klein is NOT happy with Tina and me for skipping yesterday.

Of course I told her we didn't skip, that we had a medical emergency that necessitated a trip to Ho's (for Tampax), but I am not sure Mademoiselle Klein believes me. You would think she would show some feminine solidarity with the whole surfing-the-crimson-wave thing, but apparently not. At least she didn't write us up. She let us off with a warning and assigned us a five-hundred-word essay each (in French, of course) about snails.

But that isn't even what I want to write about. What I want to write about is this:

MY DAD RULES!!!!!

And not just a country, either. He totally got me out of the contessa's black-and-white ball!!!!

What happened was – at least according to Mr G, who just caught me outside in the hall and filled me in – the filibuster over the parking fees was finally broken (after thirty-six hours) and my mom was finally able to get through to my dad (those in favour of charging for parking won. It is a victory for the environment as well as the Genovian Historical Society, who felt that many of our narrower streets would not be able to withstand the rumble of recreational vehicles that would ensue if we allowed free parking).

Anyway, my dad fully said that I did not have to go to the contessa's party. Not only that, but he said he had never heard anything so ridiculous in his life, that the only feud going on between our family and the royal family of Monaco is Grandmere's. Apparently she and the contessa have been in competition since finishing school, and Grandmere had just wanted to show off her granddaughter, about whom books and movies have been made. Apparently the contessa's only granddaughter is in rehab in Fresno, so you can sort of see where Grandmere was coming from, although, of course, what she'd been trying to do isn't very nice.

So I am free! Free to spend tomorrow night with my only love! I cat-on-the-roofed Michael for nothing! Everything is going to be all right, despite my lack of lucky underwear, I can feel it in my bones.

I am so happy, I feel like writing a poem. I will shield it from Tina, however, because it is unseemly to gloat over one's own fortunes when the fortunes of another are so exceedingly wretched (Tina found out who Jasmine is: a girl who goes to Trinity, with Dave. Her father is an oil sheikh, too. Jasmine has aquamarine braces and her screenname is IluvJustin2345).

Homework:

Algebra: probs at end of Chapt. 11
English: in journal, describe feelings pertaining to reading John Donne's *The Bait*
Biology: Don't know, Shameeka is doing it for me
Health and Safety: Chapter 2: Environmental Hazards and You
G & T: figure out secret talent
French: Chapitre Onze, ecrivez une narratif, 300 words, double space, plus 500 wds on snails
World Civ.: 500 wds, describe origins of Armenian conflict

Poem for Michael

Oh, Michael,
soon we'll be parkin'
in front of Grand Moff Tarkin
Enjoying veggie moo shu
to the beeps of R2D2
And maybe even holding hands
while gazing upon the Tatooine sands
And knowing that our love by far
has more fire power than the Death Star
And though they may blow up our planet
and kill every creature living on it
Like Leia and Han, in the stars above,
they can never destroy our love—
Like the Millennium Falcon in hyperdrive
our love will continue to thrive and thrive.

Thursday, January 21, Limo on Way Home from Grandmere's

It takes a big person to admit she's wrong – Grandmere is the one who taught me that.

And if it's true, then I must be even bigger than my five feet nine inches. Because I've been wrong. I've been wrong about Grandmere. All this time, when I thought she was inhuman and perhaps even sent down from an alien mothership to observe life on this planet and then report back to her superiors. Yeah, it turns out Grandmere really is human, just like me.

How did I find this out? How did I discover that the Dowager Princess of Genovia did not, after all, sell her soul to the Prince of Darkness as I have often surmised?

I learned it today when I walked into Grandmere's suite at the Plaza, fully prepared to do battle with her over the whole Contessa Trevanni thing. I was going to be all, 'Grandmere, Dad says I don't have to go, and guess what, I'm not going to.'

That's what I was going to say, anyway.

Except that when I walked in and saw her, the words practically died on my lips. Because Grandmere looked as if someone had run over her with a truck! Seriously. She was sitting there in the dark – she had had these purple scarves thrown over the lampshades because she said the light was hurting her eyes – and she wasn't even dressed properly. She had on a velvet lounging robe, a cashmere throw over her knees and some slippers and that was it, and her hair was all in curlers and if her eyeliner hadn't been tattooed on, I swear it would have been all smeared. She wasn't even enjoying a Sidecar, her favourite refreshment, or anything.

She was just sitting there, with Rommel trembling on her lap, looking like death warmed over.

'Grandmere,' I couldn't help crying out, when I saw her. 'Are you all right? Are you sick or something? Do you want me to get your maid?'

But all Grandmere said was, in a voice so unlike her own normally quite strident one that I could barely believe it belonged to the same woman, 'No, I'm fine. At least I will be. Once I get over the humiliation.'

'Humiliation? What humiliation?' I went over to kneel by her chair. 'Grandmere, are you sure you aren't sick? You aren't even smoking!'

'I'll be all right,' she said, weakly. 'It will be weeks before I'll be able to show my face in public. But I'm a Renaldo. I'm strong. I will recover.'

Actually, Grandmere is technically only a Renaldo by marriage, but at that point I wasn't going to argue with her, because I thought there was something genuinely wrong, like her uterus had fallen out in the shower or something (this happened to one of the women in the condo community down in Boca where Lilly and Michael's grandmother lives).

'Grandmere,' I said, kind of looking around, in case her uterus was lying on the floor somewhere or whatever. 'Do you want me to call a doctor?'

'No doctor can cure what is wrong with me,' Grandmere assured me. 'I am only suffering from the mortification of having a granddaughter who doesn't love me.'

I had no idea what she was talking about. Sure, I don't like Grandmere so much sometimes. Sometimes I even think I hate her. But I don't not love her. I guess. At least I've never said so, to her face.

'Grandmere, what are you talking about? Of course I love you . . .'

157

'Then why won't you come with me to the Contessa Trevanni's black-and-white ball?' Grandmere wailed.

Blinking rapidly, I could only stammer, 'Wh-what?'

'Your father says you will not go to the ball,' Grandmere said. 'He says you have no wish to go!'

'Grandmere,' I said. 'You know I don't want to go. You know that Michael and—'

'*That boy!*' Grandmere cried. '*That boy* again!'

'Grandmere, stop calling him that,' I said. 'You know his name perfectly well. It's Michael.'

'And I suppose this Michael,' Grandmere said, 'is more important to you than *I* am. I suppose you consider his feelings over mine in this case.'

The answer to that, of course, was a resounding *yes*. But I didn't want to be rude. I said, 'Grandmere, tomorrow night is our first date. Mine and Michael's, I mean. It's really important to me.'

'And I suppose the fact that it was really important to *me* that you attend this ball – that is of no consequence?' Grandmere actually looked, for a moment, as she sat gazing down at me so miserably, as if she had tears in her eyes. But maybe it was only a trick of the not very clear light. 'The fact that Elena Trevanni has, ever since I was a little girl, always lorded it over me, because she was born into a more respected and aristocratic family than I was? That until I married your grandfather, she always had nicer clothes and shoes and handbags than my parents could afford for me? That she still thinks she is so much better than me, because she married a comte who had no responsibilities or property, just unlimited wealth, whereas I have been forced to work my fingers to the bone in order to make Genovia the vacation paradise it is today? And that I was hoping that just this

158

once, by revealing what a lovely and accomplished grand-daughter I have, I could show her up?'

I was stunned. I'd had no idea why this stupid ball was so important to her. I thought it had just been because she'd wanted to try to split Michael and me up, or get me to start liking Prince René instead, so that the two of us could unite our families in holy matrimony someday and create a race of super-royals. It had never occurred to me that there might be some underlying, mitigating circumstance . . .

. . . such as that the Contessa Trevanni was, in essence, Grandmere's Lana Weinberger.

Because that's what it sounded like. Like Elena Trevanni had tortured and teased Grandmere as mercilessly as I had been tortured and teased by Lana through the years.

I wondered if Elena, like Lana, had ever suggested to Grandmere that she wear Band-Aids on her boobs instead of a bra. If she had, she was a far, far braver soul than I.

'And now,' Grandmere said, very sadly, 'I have to tell her that my granddaughter doesn't love me enough to put aside her new boyfriend for one single night.'

I realized, with a sinking heart, what I had to do. I mean, I knew how Grandmere felt. If there had been some way, any way at all, that I could have shown up Lana – you know, besides going out with her boyfriend, which I had already done, but that had ended up humiliating *me* way more than it had Lana – I'd have done it. Anything.

Because when someone is as mean and cruel and just downright nasty as Lana is – not just to me, either, but to all the girls at Albert Einstein High who aren't blessed with good looks and school spirit – she fully deserves to have her nose rubbed in it.

It was so weird to think about someone like Grandmere, who seemed so incredibly sure of herself, having a Lana

Weinberger in her life. I mean, I had always pictured Grandmere being the type of person who, if Lana flipped her long blonde on to her desk, would go all *Crouching Tiger* on her and deliver a kick to the face.

But maybe there was someone even Grandmere was a little bit afraid of. And maybe that person was Contessa Trevanni.

And while it is not true that I love Grandmere more than I love Michael – I do not love anyone more than I love Michael, except of course for Fat Louie – I did feel sorrier for Grandmere at that moment than I did for myself. You know, if Michael ended up dumping me because I cancelled our date. It sounds incredible, but it's true.

So I went, even as I said them, not quite believing the words were coming out of my mouth, 'All right, Grandmere, I'll put in an appearance at your ball.'

A miraculous change overcame Grandmere. She seemed to brighten right up.

'Really, Amelia?' she asked, reaching out to grasp one of my hands. 'Will you really do this for me?'

I was, I knew, going to lose Michael forever. But like my mother had said, if he didn't understand then he probably hadn't been right for me in the first place.

Yeah, right!!! Michael is the most perfect guy in the universe!! Our astrological charts even prove it!!! And I was throwing it all away for Grandmere, whom I am pretty sure I don't even like!!!

God, I am such a pushover. But she just looked so happy. She flung off the cashmere throw, and Rommel, and rang for her maid to bring her a Sidecar and her cigarettes, and then we moved on to the day's lesson – how to cheat at canasta without being found out, a necessity during games with the highly volatile Bengazi royal family, who, if they aren't allowed to win, tend to go out the next day and raze entire villages.

All I want to know is: What?

Not about the Bengazis.

I mean what – WHAT???? – am I going to tell Michael? I mean, seriously. If he doesn't dump me now then there's something wrong with him. And since I know there is nothing wrong with him, I know that I am about to be dumped.

About which all I can say is THERE IS NO JUSTICE IN THE WORLD. NONE.

Since Lilly has her breakfast meeting with the producers of the made-for-TV movie of my life tomorrow morning, I guess I will break the news to Michael then. That way he can dump me in time for Homeroom. Maybe then I will have stopped crying before Lana sees me in Algebra second period. I don't think I'll be able to take her mockery, after already having my heart ripped from my body and flung across the floor.

I hate myself.

Thursday, January 21, the Loft

I saw the movie of my life. My mom taped it for me while I was in Genovia. She thought Mr G recorded *Temptation Island* over it, but it turned out he didn't.

The girl who played me was way prettier than I am in real life. My mom says that's not true, but I know it is.

I guess I can see why Lilly is so mad, though. I mean, her character wasn't exactly supportive of mine for a good two-thirds of the movie.

The guy who played Michael was a total babe. In the movie, he and I end up together.

Too bad in real life he is going to dump me tomorrow . . . even though Tina doesn't think so.

This is very nice of her, and everything, but the fact is, he is totally going to. I mean, it really is a matter of pride. If a girl with whom you have been going out for a full thirty-four days cancels your very first date, you really have no choice but to break up with her. I mean, I totally understand. *I* would break up with me. It is clear now that royal teens can't be like normal ones. I mean, for people like me and Prince William, duty will always have to come first. Who is going to be able to understand that, let alone put up with it?

Tina says Michael can, and will. Tina says Michael won't break up with me because he loves me. I said yes he will, because he only loves me as a friend.

'Clearly Michael loves you as more than just a friend,' Tina keeps saying into the phone. 'I mean, you guys kissed!'

'Yes,' I say. 'But Kenny and I kissed, and I did not like him as more than just a friend.'

'This is a completely different situation,' Tina says.

'How?'

'Because you and Michael are meant to be together!' Tina sounds exasperated. 'Your star chart says so! You and Kenny were never meant for one another, he is a Cancer.'

Tina's astrological predictions notwithstanding, there is no evidence that Michael feels more strongly for me than he does for, say, Judith Gershner. Yes, he wrote me that poem that mentioned the L word. But that was an entire month ago, during which period I was in another country. He has not renewed any such protestations since my return. I think it highly likely that tomorrow will be the straw that breaks the hot guy's back. I mean, why would Michael waste his time on a girl like me, who can't even stand up to her own grandmother? I'm sure if Michael's grandmother had been all, 'Michael, you've got to go to bingo with me Friday night, because Olga Krakowski, my childhood rival, will be there, and I want to show you off,' he'd have been all, 'Sorry, Gran, no can do.'

No, I'm the spineless one. I'm the one completely lacking in backbone.

And I'm the one who now must suffer for it.

I wonder if it is too late in the school year to transfer. Because I really don't think I can take going to the same school as Michael after we are broken up. Seeing him in the hallway between classes, at lunch, and in G and T, knowing he was once mine but that I'd lost him, might just kill me.

But is there another school in Manhattan that might take a talentless, backbone-lacking reject like myself? Doubtful.

For Michael

Oh, Michael, my one true love
We had all new pleasures yet to prove
But I lost you due to my own retardation
before our love had yet found fru-ation
And now through the years, for you I will pine
and mourn for the days when you were once mine.

Friday, January 22, Homeroom

Well. That's it. It's over. He dumped me.

All right, not in so many words. But I could see it in his face.

He tried to be nice about it. I mean, he didn't come right out and say, 'Get back, Jack.'

But I could see it in his eyes.

'No, really, Mia,' was what he said. 'I understand. You're a princess. Duty comes first.'

That is what he said. What he meant was:

'Hmmm, I wonder if Judith Gershner has broken up with that guy from Trinity yet? Maybe she's available, since this loser Mia sure isn't.'

I told him that I would try to get out of the ball early if I could. He said that if I did, I should stop by. The Moscovitzes' apartment, I mean.

I know what this means, of course:

That he is going to dump me there.

Because he can't dump me in my own limo, in front of my bodyguard and driver. I mean, for all Michael knows, Lars might be trained to beat up boys who try to dump me in front of him. Surely Michael, having a normal sense of self-preservation, will choose to break off our relationship in the privacy of his own home, where he will be safe from rubber bullets and ninja throwing stars.

I cannot blame him. I would do the same thing.

Now I know how Jane Eyre must have felt when she discovered, on her wedding day, that Mr Rochester had a wife yet living. No, Michael doesn't have a wife that I know of. But my relationship with him, like Jane's with Mr Rochester, has come to an end. And I can think of no earthly way it can ever be repaired. I mean, it's possible that tonight, when I go by the Moscovitzes' place, it will be in flames, and I will be able to prove myself worthy of Michael's love by selflessly saving his mother, or perhaps his dog, Pavlov, from the fire.

But other than that, I don't see us getting back together. I will, of course, give him his birthday present, because I went to all the trouble of stealing it.

But I know it won't do any good. It's over. Like my life.

They just announced the name of the newest member of the Albert Einstein High junior varsity cheerleading squad. It is Shameeka Taylor.

Who even cares?

Friday, January 22, Algebra

Michael did not stop by here between classes. It is the first day all week that he hasn't slipped in to say hi on his way to Senior English, three classrooms away from this one.

It is obvious why. I mean, we are broken up. He hates me now. I don't blame him. I hate myself.

To make matters worse – as if I can even care about something so trivial – Lana just turned around to hiss, 'Don't think just because your little friend made the squad that anything is going to change between us, Mia. She's as much of a pathetic geekette as you are. They only let her on the squad to fulfil our freak quota.'

Then she whipped her head around again – but not as fast as she should have. Because a lot of her hair was still draped across my desk.

And when I slammed my Algebra I–II text closed as hard as I could – which is what I did next – a lot of her silky, awa-puhi-scented locks got trapped between page 212 and 213.

Lana shrieked in pain. Mr G, up at the chalkboard, turned around, saw where the screaming was coming from, and sighed.

'Mia,' he said, tiredly, 'Lana. What now?'

Lana stabbed an index finger in my direction. 'She slammed her book on my hair!'

I shrugged innocently. 'I didn't know her hair was in my book. Why can't she keep her hair to herself, anyway?'

Mr Gianini looked bored. 'Lana,' he said, 'if you can't keep your hair under control, I recommend braids. Mia, don't slam your book. It should be open to page two-twelve, where I want you to read from Section Two. Out loud.'

I read out loud from Section Two, but not without a certain primness. For once, vengeance on Lana had been mine, and I had NOT been sent to the principal's office. Oh, it was sweet. Sweet, sweet vindication.

Although I don't even know why I have to learn this stuff; it isn't as if the Palais de Genovia isn't full of dweeby staffers who are just dying to multiply fractions for me.

Polynomials
term: variable(s) multiplied by a coefficient
monomial: Polynomial w/ one term
binomial: Polynomial w/ two terms
trinomial: Polynomial w/ three terms
Degree of polynomial = the degree of the term with the highest degree

In my delight over the pain I had brought upon my enemy, I almost forgot about the fact that my heart is broken. Must keep in mind that Michael is dumping me after the black-and-white ball tonight. Why can't I FOCUS???? Must be love. I am sick with it.

Friday, January 22, Health and Safety

Why do you look like you just ate ANOTHER sock?

    I don't. How was your breakfast meeting?

You do, too. The meeting went GREAT.

    Really? Did they agree to print a full-page letter of apology in the Times?

No, better. Did something happen between you and my brother? Because I saw him looking all furtive in the hallway just now.

    FURTIVE? Furtive like how? Like he was looking for Judith Gershner to ask her out tonight?????

No, more like he was looking for a pay phone. Why would he ask out Judith Gershner? How many times do I have to tell you, he likes you, not J.G.

    He used to like me, you mean. Before I was forced to cancel our date tonight due to Grandmere forcing me to go to a ball.

A ball? Really. Ugh. But excuse me. Michael isn't going to ask some other girl to go out with him tonight just because you can't make it. I mean, he was really looking forward to going with you. Not just for concupiscent reasons, either.

    REALLY?????

Yes, you loser. What did you think? I mean, you guys are going out.

    But that's just it. We haven't. Gone out yet, I mean.

So? You'll go out sometime when you don't have a ball to go to instead.

    You don't think he's going to dump me?

Uh, not unless something heavy fell on his head between now and the last time I saw him. Guys with cranial damage can't generally be held responsible for their actions.

Why would something heavy fall on his head?

I'm being facetious. Do you want to hear about my meeting, or not?

Yes. What happened?

They told me they want to option my show.

What does that mean?

It means that they will take Lilly Tells It Like It Is *around to the networks to see if anybody wants to buy it. To be a real show. On a real channel. Not like public access. Like ABC or Lifetime or VH1 or something.*

Lilly!!!! THAT IS SO GREAT!!!!

Yes, I know. Oops, gotta go, Wheeton's looking this way.

Note to self: Look up words *concupiscent* and *facetious*.

Friday, January 22, Gifted and Talented

Lunch was just one big celebration today. Everyone had something to be happy about:

- Shameeka, for making the cheerleading squad and striking a blow for tall geeky girls everywhere (even though, of course, Shameeka looks like a supermodel and can wrap both her ankles around her head, but, whatever).
- Lilly, for getting her TV show optioned.
- Tina, for finally deciding to give up on Dave, but not on romance in general, and get on with her life.
- Ling Su for getting her drawing of Joe, the stone lion, into the school art fair.
- And Boris for just, well, being Boris. Boris is always happy.

You will notice that I did not mention Michael. That is because I do not know what Michael's mental state at lunch was, whether or not he was happy or sad or concupiscent or whatever. That is because Michael didn't show up to lunch. He said, when he breezed by my locker just before fourth period, 'Hey, I've got some things to do, I'll see you in G and T, OK?'

Some things to do. Like, for instance, find another girl to take to the movie tonight.

I should, of course, just ask him. I should just be like, *Look, are we broken up, or what?* Because I would really like to know, one way or the other, so I can begin planning either my wedding or my funeral.

Well, not really, because, of course, I don't live in Utah, and I would never kill myself over a boy, even Michael. But you know what I mean.

Except that I can't just go up and ask Michael what the deal is between us, because right now he is busy with Boris, going over band stuff. Michael's band is comprised (so far) of

Michael (bass); Boris (electric violin); that tall guy Paul from the Computer Club (keyboards); this guy from the AEHS marching band called Trevor (guitar); and Felix, this scary-looking twelfth-grader with a goatee that's bushier than Mr Gianini's (drums). They still don't have a name for the band, or a place to practise. But they seem to think that Mr Kreblutz, the chief custodian, will let them into the band practice rooms on weekends if they can get him tickets to the Westminster Kennel Show next month. Mr Kreblutz is a huge bichon frise fan.

The fact that Michael can concentrate on all this band stuff while our relationship is falling apart is just further proof that he is a true musician, completely dedicated to his art. I, being the talentless freak that I am, can, of course, think of nothing *but* my heartbreak. Michael's ability to remain focused in spite of any personal pain he might be suffering is evidence of his genius.

Either that or he never cared that much about me in the first place.

I prefer to believe the former.

Oh, that I had some kind of outlet, such as music, into which to pour the suffering I am currently feeling! But alas, I'm no artist. I just have to sit here in silent pain, while around me more-gifted souls express their innermost angst through song, dance and filmography.

Well, OK, just through filmography since there are no singers or dancers in fifth period G and T. Though if you ask me, there should be. Instead we just have Lilly, putting together what she is calling her quintessential episode of *Lilly Tells It Like It Is*, a show that will explore the seamy underbelly of that American institution known as Starbucks. It is Lilly's contention that Starbucks, through the introduction of the Starbucks card, with which caffeine addicts can now pay for their fix electronically, is actually a secret branch of the Central Intelligence Agency that is tracing the movements of America's intelligentsia – writers, editors and other known liberal agitators – through their coffee consumption.

Whatever. I don't even like coffee.

This can't be how it ends, can it? My love affair with Michael, I mean. Not with a bang, but with hardly even a whimper, like Rommel when you accidentally step on his tail?

This so isn't how Mr Rochester would have done it. Broken up with Jane, I mean. If he'd decided to break up with her. Which he never did because he loved her too much, even when she ran away from him and went to go live with another guy. Well, OK, and his sisters, and he turned out to be her cousin, but, whatever.

No, even then Mr Rochester reached out psychically and touched Jane's mind with his. Because though their bodies might be parted, their souls were forever entwined by a love that was stronger than—

Aw, crud. The bell.

Homework:
Algebra: Who cares?
English: Everything sucks.
Biology: I hate life.
Health and Safety: Mr Wheeton is in love, too. I should warn him to get out now, while he still can.
G & T: I shouldn't even be in this class.
French: Why does this language even exist? Everyone there speaks English anyway.
World Civ.: What does it matter? We're all just going to die. Once our boyfriends dump us, anyway.

173

Friday, January 22, 6 p.m. Grandmere's Suite at the Plaza

Grandmere made me come here straight after school so that Paolo could start getting us ready for the ball. I didn't know Paolo makes housecalls, but apparently he does. Only for royalty, he assured me, and Britney.

I explained to him about how I am growing out my hair on account of boys liking long hair better than short hair, and Paolo made some tut-tutting noises, but he slapped some curlers into it to try to get rid of the triangular shape, and I guess it worked, because my hair looks pretty good. All of me looks pretty good. On the outside, anyway.

Too bad inside, I'm completely busted.

I am trying not to show it, though. You know, because I want Grandmere to think I am having a good time. I mean, I am only doing this for her. Because she is an old lady and my grandmother and she fought the Nazis and all of that, for which someone has to give her some credit.

I just hope someday she appreciates it. My supreme sacrifice, I mean. But I doubt she ever will. Seventy-something-year-old ladies – particularly dowager princesses – never seem to remember what it was like to be fourteen and in love.

Well, I guess it is time to go. Grandmere has on this slinky black number with glitter all over it. She looks like Diana Ross. Only with no eyebrows.

She says I look like a snowdrop. Hmmm, just what I always wanted, to look like a snowdrop.

Maybe that's my secret talent. I have the amazing ability to resemble a snowdrop.

My parents must be so proud.

Friday, January 22, 8 p.m. Bathroom at the Contessa Trevanni's Fifth-Avenue Mansion

Yep. In the bathroom once again, where I always seem to end up at dances. Why is that?

The contessa's bathroom is a little bit overdone. It is nice and everything, but I don't know if I'd have chosen flaming wall-sconces as part of my bathroom decor. I mean, even at the palace, we don't have any flaming wall-sconces. Although it looks very romantic and *Ivanhoe*-y and all, it is actually a pretty serious fire hazard, besides being probably a health risk, considering the carcinogens they must be giving off.

But, whatever. That isn't even the real question – why would anyone have flaming wall-sconces in the bathroom? The real question, of course, is this: if I am supposedly descended from all these strong women – you know, Rosagunde, who strangled that warlord with her braid, and Agnes, who jumped off that bridge, not to mention Grandmere, who allegedly kept the Nazis from trashing Genovia by having Hitler over for tea – why is it that I am such a pushover?

I mean, seriously. I totally fell for Grandmere's whole riff about wanting to show up Elena Trevanni with her pretty and accomplished – yeah, at looking like a snowdrop – granddaughter. I actually felt sorry for her. I had empathy for Grandmere, not realizing then – as I do now – that Grandmere is completely devoid of human emotion, and that the whole thing was just a charade to trick me into coming so she could parade me around as PRINCE RENÉ'S NEW GIRLFRIEND!!!!!!!!!!!!!!!

To his credit, René seems to have known nothing about it.

175

He looked as surprised as I was when Grandmere presented me to her supposed arch-rival, who, thanks to the skill of Lana's plastic surgeon dad, looks about thirty years younger than Grandmere, though they are supposedly the same age.

But I think the contessa maybe went a little far with the surgery thing – it is so hard to know when to say 'when', I mean, look at poor Michael Jackson – because she really does, just like Grandmere said, resemble an anteater. Like her eyes are sort of far apart on account of the skin around them being stretched so tight, which makes her nose look extra long and skinny.

When Grandmere introduced me – 'Contessa, may I present to you my granddaughter, Princess Amelia Mignonette Grimaldi Renaldo' (she always leaves out the Thermopolis) – I thought everything was going to be all right. Well, not everything, of course, since directly after the ball, I knew I was going to go over to my best friend's house and get dumped by her brother. But you know, everything at the ball.

But then Grandmere added, 'And of course you know Amelia's beau, Prince Pierre René Grimaldi Alberto.'

Beau? BEAU??? René and I exchanged quick glances. It was only then that I noticed that, standing right behind us in the reception line was none other than Lana Weinberger, her dad, and her mom. RIGHT THERE BEHIND US.

And Lana's mom, I saw, had allowed Lana to wear black instead of white to the black-and-white ball, even though I had been told, on no uncertain terms, that it was unseemly for a girl of my tender years to wear black. And Lana is the same age as me.

Lana, of course, totally overheard Grandmere's remark about me and René, and she got this look on her face . . .

Well, let's just say I'm surprised she didn't pull out her mobile then and there and call everyone she knew to tell them that Mia Thermopolis was two-timing her best friend's brother.

So while I was standing there getting totally red in the face, and probably not resembling a snowdrop any more as much as a candy cane, the contessa looked down her foot-long nose at me and went, 'So that rascal René has finally been snatched up, and by your granddaughter, Clarisse. How satisfying that must be for you.'

Then Grandmere said, 'Isn't it, though, Elena?' And then to René and me she went, 'Come along, children,' and we followed her, René looking amused. But me? I was seething.

'I can't believe you did that,' I cried, as soon as we were out of the contessa's earshot.

'Did what, Amelia?' Grandmere asked, nodding to some guy in traditional African garb – a member of the Bengazi royal family, no doubt.

'Told that woman that René and I are going out,' I said, 'when we most certainly are not. Grandmere, how many times do I have to tell you, I'm going out with Michael Moscovitz!' At least I was until tonight, anyway.

'René,' Grandmere said, sweetly. She can be very sweet when she wants to be. 'Be an angel and see if you can find us some champagne, would you?'

René, still looking cynically amused – the way I imagined Mr Rochester must have looked a lot of the time before he went blind and got his hand chopped off – moved off in search of libation.

'Really, Amelia,' Grandmere said, when he was gone. 'Must you be so rude to poor René? I am only trying to make your cousin feel welcome and at home.'

'There is a difference,' I said, 'between making my cousin

feel welcome and wanted, and trying to pass him off as my boyfriend!'

'Well, what's so wrong with René, anyway?' Grandmere wanted to know. All around us, elegant people in tuxedos and evening gowns were heading to the dance floor, where a full orchestra was playing that song Audrey Hepburn sang in that movie about Tiffany's. Everyone was dressed in either black or white or both. The contessa's ballroom bore a significant resemblance to the penguin enclosure at the Central Park Zoo, where I had once sobbed my eyes out after discovering the truth about my heritage.

'He's extremely charming,' Grandmere went on, 'and quite cosmopolitan. Not to mention devilishly handsome. How can you possibly prefer a high school boy to a *prince*?'

'Because, Grandmere,' I said, 'I love him.'

'Love,' Grandmere said, looking towards the big glass ceiling overhead. *'Pfuit!'*

'Yes, Grandmere,' I said. 'I do. The way you loved Grandpere – and don't try to deny it, because I know you did. Now you've got to stop harbouring a secret desire to make Prince René your grandson-in-law, because it is not going to happen.'

Grandmere looked blandly innocent. 'I don't know what you can mean,' she said, with a sniff.

'Cut it out, Grandmere. You want me to marry Prince René, for no other reason than that he is a royal. Well, it isn't going to happen. Even if Michael and I were to break up . . .' which was going to happen sooner than she thought '. . . I wouldn't get together with René. He's not my type. He smokes. And he likes to gamble. And he has no sympathy whatsoever for the plight of the giant sea turtle.'

Grandmere finally began to look as if she might believe me. 'Fine,' she said, without much grace. 'I will stop calling

René your beau. But you must dance with him. At least once.'

'Grandmere.' The last thing in the world I felt like was dancing. 'Please. Not tonight. You don't know—'

'Amelia,' Grandmere said, in a different tone of voice from the one she'd used thus far. 'One dance. That is all I am asking for. I believe you owe it to me.'

'*I* owe it to *you*?' I couldn't help bursting out laughing at that one. 'How so?'

'Oh, only because of a little something,' Grandmere said, all innocently, 'that was recently found to be missing from the palace museum.'

All of my Renaldo fighting spirit went right out the contessa's French doors to her backyard patio when I heard this. I felt as if someone had punched me in my snowdrop stomach. Had Grandmere really said what I *thought* she'd said???

Swallowing hard, I went, 'Wh-what?'

'Yes.' Grandmere looked at me meaningfully. 'A priceless object – one out of a group of several, almost identical items that was given to me by my very dear friend, Mr Richard Nixon, the deceased former American president – has been found to be missing. I realize the person who took it thought it would never be missed, because it wasn't the only such item, and they all did look much alike. Still, it held great sentimental value for me. Dick was such a dear, sweet friend to Genovia while he was in office, for all his later troubles. *But you wouldn't happen to know anything about any of this, would you, Amelia?*'

She had me! She had me, and she knew it. I don't know how she knew – undoubtedly through the black arts, in which I suspect Grandmere of being highly well-versed – but clearly, she knew. I was dead. I was so, so dead. I don't know if, being a member of the royal family, and all, I was

179

above the law back in Genovia, but I for one did not want to find out.

I should, I realize now, merely have dissembled. I should have been all, 'Priceless object? What priceless object?'

But I couldn't, on account of my nostrils. Instead, I went, in this squeaky, high-pitched voice I barely recognized as my own, 'You know what, Grandmere? I'll be happy to dance with René. No problem!'

Grandmere looked extremely satisfied. She said, 'Yes, I thought you would feel that way.' Then her drawn-on eyebrows went up. 'Oh, look, here comes Prince René with our drinks. Sweet of him, don't you think?'

Anyway, that's how it happened that I was forced to dance with Prince René – who is a good dancer, but, whatever, he's no Michael. I mean, he's never even seen *Buffy the Vampire Slayer* and he thinks Bill Gates is a pretty swell guy.

While we were dancing, though, this incredible thing happened. René went, 'Who is this blonde girl who keeps staring at us? Do you know her?'

I looked over to see who he was talking about, and sure enough, Lana was dancing nearby with some old guy who must have been a friend of her father's. She looked extremely pained, like the old guy was talking to her about his investment portfolio or something, and, I have to admit, the looks she was throwing in my direction were pretty envious.

Well, I guess, to a girl like Lana, I was in an enviable position. I looked like a snowdrop, and I was dancing with the handsomest guy in the room. Too bad I was in love with somebody else.

So then, I don't know what came over me, but I actually sort of started feeling sorry for Lana. I mean, she's so shallow. She can't see past how somebody looks. She never

180

bothers to stop and try to see the person they might be inside.

I don't know, maybe being the daughter of a plastic surgeon makes her insecure, or something. But it's like, if you don't look or dress a certain way, Lana won't even give you the time of day.

And yeah, I knew that on Monday she was going to be going around school, telling everybody she could get to listen about how she saw me with another guy. But by that time Michael and I would be broken up anyway. So what did it matter?

So for the second time in two days, I did something because I felt sorry for someone whom I'd formerly considered pretty much an enemy. I looked up at René and said, 'Yeah, I know her. Her name is Lana. She goes to my school. When this dance is over, you should ask her for the next one.'

René looked dubious. 'Really?'

'Trust me,' I said. 'It'll be the thrill of her life to dance with a handsome prince.'

'But not so much for you, eh,' René said, still wearing his cynical smile.

'René,' I said. 'No offence. But I already met my prince, long before I ever met you. The only problem is, if I don't get out of here soon, I don't know how much longer he's going to be my prince, because I already missed the movie we were supposed to see together, and pretty soon it's going to be too late even for me to stop by . . .'

'Never fear, Your Highness,' René said, twirling me around. 'If fleeing the ball before the clock strikes twelve is your desire, I will see to it that your wish is fulfilled.'

I looked at him kind of dubiously. I actually needed to get out of the ball by nine, not twelve, if I still wanted to make it to Michael's at a decent hour. Also, I couldn't tell whether or not René was joking.

'Um,' I said. 'OK.'

And that's how I ended up in this bathroom. René told me to hide, and that he'd get Lars to flag down a cab, and once he'd got one, and the coast was clear, René would knock three times, signalling that Grandmere was too otherwise occupied to notice my defection. Then, René promised, he'd tell her I must have eaten a bad truffle, since I'd looked queasy, and Lars had taken me home.

It doesn't matter, of course. Any of this, I mean. Because I am just going to end up at Michael's in time for him to dump me. Maybe he'll feel bad about it, you know, after I give him his birthday present. Then again, maybe he'll just be glad to be rid of me. Who knows? I've given up trying to figure out men. They are a breed apart.

Oops, there's René's knock. Gotta go.

To meet my fate.

Friday, January 22, 11 p.m. The Moscovitzes' Bathroom

Oh, my God, I am FREAKING OUT.

Now I know how Jane Eyre must have felt when she returned to Thornfield Hall to find it all burnt to the ground and everyone telling her everybody inside of it was killed in the fire.

Only then she finds out Mr Rochester didn't die, he just lost his sight and his hand and his crazy wife and everything, and Jane's like super happy, because, you know, in spite of what he tried to do to her, she loves him.

That's how I feel right now. Super happy. Because I fully don't think Michael is going to break up with me after all!!!!

I was sure he was going to when I was standing outside the Moscovitzes' apartment, you know, with my finger on the buzzer. I was standing there going, *Why am I even doing this? I am fully just walking into heartbreak. I should turn around and have Lars flag down another cab and just go back to the loft.* I hadn't even bothered changing out of my stupid ball gown, because what was the point? I was just going to be on my way home in a few minutes anyway, and I could change there.

So I'm standing there in the hallway, and Lars is behind me going on about his stupid boar hunt in Belize, because that is all he talks about any more, and I hear Pavlov, Michael's dog, barking because someone is at the door, and I'm going, inside my head, *OK, when he breaks up with me, I am NOT going to cry, I am going to remember Rosagunde and Agnes, and I am going to be strong like they were strong . . .*

And then Michael opened the door. He looked kind of

taken aback by my apparel, I could tell. I thought maybe it was because he hadn't counted on having to break up with a snowdrop. But there was nothing I could do about that, though I did remember at the last minute that I was still wearing my tiara, which I suppose might intimidate, you know, some boys.

So I took it off and went, 'Well, I'm here,' which is a foolish thing to say, because, well, duh, I was standing there, wasn't I?

But Michael kind of seemed to recover himself. He went, 'Oh, hey, come in, you look . . . you look really beautiful,' which of course is exactly what a guy who is about to break up with you would say, you know, to kind of bolster your ego before he grinds it beneath his heel.

But, whatever, I went in, and so did Lars, and Michael went, 'Lars, my mom and dad are in the living room watching *Dateline*, if you want to join them,' which Lars totally did, because you could tell he didn't want to hang around and listen to the Big Breakup.

So then Michael and I were alone in the foyer. I was twirling my tiara around in my hands, trying to think of what to say. I'd been trying to think what to say the whole way down in the cab, but I hadn't been very successful.

Then Michael went, 'Well, did you eat yet? Because I've got some veggie burgers . . .'

I looked up from the parquet floor tiles, which I had been examining very closely, since it was easier than looking into Michael's peat-bog eyes, which always suck me in until I feel like I can't move any more. They used to punish criminals in ancient Celtic societies by making them walk into a peat bog. If they sank, you know, they were guilty, and if not, they were innocent. Only you always sink when you walk into a peat bog. They uncovered a bunch of bodies from one in

Ireland not too long ago, and they, like, still had all their teeth and hair and stuff. They were totally preserved. It was way gross.

That's how I feel when I look into Michael's eyes. Like I'm trapped in peat bog. Only I don't mind, because it's warm and nice and cosy in there . . .

And now he was asking me if I wanted a veggie burger. Do guys generally ask their girlfriends if they want a veggie burger right before they break up with them? I wasn't very well versed in these matters, so the truth was, I didn't know.

But I didn't think so.

'Um,' I said, intelligently. 'I don't know.' I thought maybe it was a trick question. 'If you're having one, I guess.'

So then Michael went, 'OK,' and gestured for me to follow him, and we went into the kitchen, where Lilly was sitting, using the granite countertop to lay out her story-boards for the episode of *Lilly Tells It Like It Is* she was filming the next day.

'Jeez,' she said, when she saw me. 'What happened to you? You look like you swapped outfits with the Sugar Plum Fairy.'

'I was at a ball,' I explained.

'Oh,' Lilly said, 'of course. The ball. Well, if you ask me, the Sugar Plum Fairy got the better deal. But I'm not supposed to be here. So don't mind me.'

'We won't,' Michael assured her.

And then he did the strangest thing. He started to cook.

Seriously. He was *cooking*.

Well, OK, not really cooking, more like reheating. Still, he fully got out these two veggie burgers he'd gotten from Balducci's, and put them on some buns, and then put the buns on these two plates. And then he took some fries that had been in the oven on a tray and put them on to the two

185

plates, as well. And then he got ketchup and mayo and mustard out of the fridge, along with two cans of Coke, and he put all that stuff on a tray, and then he walked out of the kitchen, and before I could ask Lilly what in the name of all that was holy was going on, he came back, picked up the two plates, and went, to me, 'Come on.'

What could I do, but follow him?

I trailed after him into the TV room, where Lilly and I had viewed so many cinematic gems for the first time, such as *Valley Girl* and *Bring It On* and *Attack of the Fifty-Foot Woman* and *Crossing Delancey*.

And there, in front of the Moscovitzes' black leather couch, which sat in front of their thirty-two-inch Sony TV, sat two little folding tables. On to these tables, Michael lowered the plates of food he'd prepared. They sat there, in the glow of the *Star Wars* title image, which was frozen on the TV screen, obviously paused there.

'Michael,' I said, genuinely baffled. 'What *is* this?'

'Well, you couldn't make it to the Screening Room,' he said, looking as if he couldn't quite believe I hadn't figured it out on my own yet. 'So I brought the Screening Room to you. Come on, let's eat. I'm starved.'

He might have been starved, but I was stunned. I stood there looking down at the veggie burgers – which smelt divine – going, 'Wait a minute. Wait a minute. You aren't breaking up with me?'

Michael had already sat down on the couch and stuffed a few fries in his mouth. When I said that, about breaking up, he turned around to look at me like I was demented. 'Break up with you? Why would I do that?'

'Well,' I said, starting to wonder if maybe he was right, and I really *was* demented. 'When I told you I couldn't make it tonight you . . . well, you seemed kind of distant . . .'

186

'I wasn't distant,' Michael said. 'I was trying to figure out what we could do instead of, you know, going to the movie.'

'But then you didn't show up for lunch . . .'

'Right,' Michael said. 'I had to call and order the veggie burgers and get Maya to go to the store and get the rest of the stuff. And my dad had loaned our *Star Wars* DVD to a friend of his, so I had to call him and make him get it back.'

I listened in astonishment. Everyone, it seemed – Maya, the Moscovitzes' housekeeper; Lilly; even Michael's parents – had been in on Michael's scheme to recreate the Screening Room right in his own apartment.

Only I had been in ignorance of his plan. Just as he had been in ignorance of my belief that he was about to break up with me.

'Oh,' I said, beginning to feel like the world's number one biggest dork. 'So . . . you don't want to break up?'

'No, I don't want to break up,' Michael said, starting to look mad now – probably the way Mr Rochester looked when he heard Jane had been hanging out with that St John guy. 'Mia, I love you, remember? Why would I want to break up with you? Now come and sit down and eat before it gets cold.'

Then I wasn't *beginning* to feel like the world's biggest dork: I *totally* felt like it.

But at the same time, I felt incredibly, blissfully happy. Because Michael had said the L word! Said it right to my face! And in a very bossy way, just like Captain Von Trapp or the Beast or Patrick Swayze!

Then Michael hit the play button on the remote, and the first chords of John Williams's brilliant *Star Wars* theme filled the room. And Michael went, 'Mia, come on. Unless you want to change out of that dress first. Did you bring any normal clothes?'

187

Still, something wasn't right. Not completely.

'Do you just love me like a friend?' I asked him, trying to sound cynically amused, you know, the way René would, in order to keep the truth from him – that my heart was pounding a mile a minute. 'Or are you *in* love with me?'

Michael was staring over the back of the couch at me. He looked like he couldn't quite believe his ears. I couldn't believe my own. Had I really just asked him that? Just come out and asked him?

Apparently – judging from his incredulous expression, anyway – I had. I could feel myself starting to turn redder, and redder, and redder, and redder . . .

Jane Eyre would so never have asked that question.

But then again, maybe she ought to have. Because the way Michael responded made the whole embarrassment of having had to ask completely and totally worth it. And the way he responded was, he reached out, took the tiara from me, laid it down on the couch beside him, took both my hands in his, pulled me down, and gave me a really long kiss.

On the lips.

Of the French variety.

We missed the entire scrolling prologue to the movie, due to kissing. Then, finally, when the sound of Princess Leia's starship being fired upon roused us from our passionate embrace, Michael said, 'Of course I'm in love with you. Now come sit down and eat.'

It truly was the most romantic moment of my entire life. If I live to be as old as Grandmere, I will never be as happy as I was at that moment. I just stood there, thrilled to pieces, for about a minute. I mean, I could barely get over it. He loved me. Not only that, he was *in* love with me! Michael Moscovitz is in love with me, Mia Thermopolis!

'Your burger is getting cold,' he said.

See? See how perfect we are for one another? He is so practical, while I have my head in the clouds. Has there ever been as perfect a couple? Has there ever been as perfect a date?

We sat there, eating our veggie burgers and watching *Star Wars*, he in his jeans and vintage Boomtown Rats T-shirt, and me in my Chanel ball gown. And when Ben Kenobi said, 'Obi Wan? That's a name I haven't heard in a long time,' we both went, right on cue, 'How long?' And Ben said, as he always does, 'A very long time.'

And when, just before Luke flies off to attack the Death Star, Michael put it on pause so he could go get dessert, I helped him clear the plates.

And then, while he was making the ice-cream sundaes, I sneaked back into the TV room, put his present on his TV table, and waited for him to come back and find it, which he did, a few minutes later.

'What's this?' he wanted to know, as he handed me my sundae, vanilla ice cream drowning in a sea of hot fudge, whipped cream and pistachios.

'It's your birthday present,' I said, barely able to contain myself, I was so excited to see what he'd think of it. It was way better than candy or a sweater. It was, I thought, the perfect gift for Michael.

I feel like I had a right to be excited, because I'd paid a pretty hefty price for Michael's gift . . . weeks of worrying about being found out, and then, after having been found out, being forced to waltz with Prince René, who was a good dancer, and all, but who kind of smelt like an ashtray.

So I was pretty stoked as Michael, with a puzzled expression on his face, sat down and picked up the box.

'I told you that you didn't have to get me anything,' he said.

189

'I know.' I was bouncing up and down, I was so excited. 'But I wanted to. And I saw this, and I thought it was *perfect*.'

'Well,' Michael said. 'Thanks.' He untied the ribbon that held the minuscule box closed, then lifted the lid . . .

And there, sitting on a wad of white cotton, it was. A dirty little rock, no bigger than an ant. Smaller than an ant, even. The size of a pinhead.

'Huh,' Michael said, looking down at the tiny speck. 'It's . . . it's really nice.'

I laughed delightedly. 'You don't even know what it is!'

'Well,' he said. 'No, I don't.'

'Can't you guess?'

'Well,' he said, again. 'It looks like . . . I mean, it closely resembles . . . a rock.'

'It *is* a rock,' I said. 'Guess where it's from.'

Michael eyed the rock. 'I don't know. Genovia?'

'No, silly,' I crowed. 'The moon! It's a moon rock! From when Neil Armstrong was up there. He collected a load of them, and then some of them got split up, and Richard Nixon gave my grandmother a bunch of them when he was in office. Well, he gave them to Genovia, technically. And I saw them and thought . . . well, that you should have one. Because I know you like space stuff. I mean how you've got the glow-in-the-dark constellations on the ceiling over your bed and all . . .'

Michael looked up from the moon rock – which he'd been staring down at like he couldn't quite believe what he was seeing – and went, 'When were you in my room?'

'Oh,' I said, feeling myself beginning to blush again. 'A long time ago . . .' Well, it had been a long time ago. It had been way back before I'd known he liked me, when I'd been sending him those anonymous love poems. '. . . once when Maya was cleaning in there.'

Michael said, 'Oh,' and looked back down at the moon rock.

'Mia,' he said, a few seconds later. 'I can't accept this.'

'Yes, you can,' I said. 'There are plenty left back at the palace museum, don't worry. Richard Nixon must have really had a thing for Grandmere, because I'm pretty sure we got more moon rocks than Monaco or anybody else.'

'Mia,' Michael said. 'It's a rock. From the *moon*.'

'Right,' I said, not certain what he was getting at. Did he not like it? It *was* kind of weird, I guess, to give your boyfriend a rock for his birthday. But it wasn't just any rock. And Michael wasn't just any boyfriend. I'd really thought he'd like it.

'It's a rock,' he said again, 'that came from two hundred and thirty-eight thousand miles away. Two hundred and thirty-eight thousand miles away from our planet.'

'Yes,' I said, wondering what I had done. I had only just gotten Michael back, after having spent a whole week convinced he was going to dump me over one thing, only to discover that he was going to dump me over something else entirely? There is seriously no justice in the world. 'Michael, if you don't like it, I can give it back. I just thought—'

'No way,' he said, moving the box out of my grasp. 'You're not getting this back. I just don't know what I'm going to get you for your birthday. This is going to be a hard act to follow.'

Was that all? I felt my blush receding.

'Oh, that,' I said. 'You can just write me another song.'

Which was kind of vixenish of me to say, because he had never admitted that song, the first one he'd ever played me, 'Tall Drink of Water', was about me. But I could tell by the

191

way he was smiling now that I'd guessed correctly. It was. It totally was.

So then we ate our sundaes and watched the rest of the movie, and when it was over and the credits were rolling, I remembered something else I'd meant to give him, something I'd thought of in the cab on the way down from the contessa's, when I'd been trying to think up what I was going to say to him if he broke up with me.

'Oh,' I said. 'I thought of a name for your band.'

'Not,' he groaned, 'the X-Wing Fighters. I beg of you.'

'No,' I said. 'Skinner Box.' Which is this thing this psychologist called Skinner had used to torture all these rats and monkeys and prove there's such a thing as a conditioned response. Pavlov, the guy Michael had named his dog after, had done the same thing, but with dogs and bells.

'Skinner Box,' Michael said, carefully.

'Yeah,' I said. 'I mean, I just figured, since you named your dog Pavlov . . .'

'I kind of like it,' Michael said. 'I'll see what the guys say.'

I beamed. The evening was turning out so much better than I had originally thought it would, I couldn't really do anything *but* beam. In fact, that's why I locked myself in the bathroom. To try to calm down a little. I am so happy, I can barely write. I—

Saturday, January 23, the Loft

Oops. I had to break off there last night, because Lilly started banging on the bathroom door, wanting to know whether I'd suddenly become bulimic or something. When I opened it (the door, I mean) and she saw me in there with my journal and my pen, and she went, all crabby (Lilly is more of a morning person than a night person), 'Do you mean to say you've been in here for the past half-hour writing in your journal?'

Which I'll admit is a little weird, but I couldn't help it. I was so happy, I HAD to write it down, so I would never forget how it felt.

'And you *still* haven't figured out what you're good at?' she asked.

When I shook my head, she just stomped away, all mad.

But I couldn't be annoyed with her, because . . . well, because I'm so in love with her brother.

The same way I can't really be mad at Grandmere, even though she did, in essence, try to foist me on to this homeless prince last night. But I can't blame her for trying. She's only trying to keep the Renaldo bloodline clean. Grandmere has obviously never studied inbreeding, like we did in Bio. last semester.

Besides, she called here a little while ago, wanting to know if I was feeling all right after the bad truffle I'd ingested. My mom, playing along, assured her that I was fine. So then Grandmere wanted to know if I could come over and have tea with her and the contessa . . . who was just dying to get to know me better. I said I was busy with homework. Which ought to impress the contessa. You know, with my diligent work ethic.

And I can't be mad at René, either, after the way he fully

193

came to my aid last night. I wonder how he and Lana got along. It would be pretty funny if she broke up with Josh on Monday, on account of finally having found her own handsome prince.

And I can't even be mad at Thompson Street Cleaners for losing my Queen Amidala underwear, because this morning there was a knock on the door to the loft, and when I opened it, our neighbour Ronnie was there with a big bag of our laundry, including Mr G's brown cords and my mom's Free Winona T-shirt. Ronnie says she must have accidentally picked up the wrong bag from the vestibule, and then she'd gone to Barbados with her boss for the holidays, and only just now noticed that she had a bag of clothing not her own.

Although I am not as happy about getting my Queen Amidala underwear back as you might think. Because, clearly, I can get along without them. I was thinking about asking for more of them for my birthday, but now I don't have to, because Michael, even though he doesn't know it, has already given me the greatest gift I've ever gotten.

And no, it's not his love – although that is probably the second greatest thing he could have given me. No, it's something that he said after Lilly went stomping away from the bathroom.

'What was that all about?' he wanted to know.

'Oh,' I said, putting away my journal, 'she's just mad because I haven't figured out what my secret talent is.'

'Your what?' Michael said.

'My secret talent.' And then, because he'd been so honest with me, about the whole being in love thing, I decided to be honest with him, too. So I explained, 'It's just that you and Lilly, you're both so talented. You guys are good at so many things, and I'm not good at anything, and sometimes I feel like . . . well, like I don't belong. At least not in Gifted and Talented class, anyway.'

'Mia,' Michael said. 'You're totally gifted.'

'Yeah,' I said, fingering my dress. 'At looking like a snow-drop.'

'No,' Michael said. 'Although now that you mention it, you're pretty good at that, too. But I meant writing.'

I have to admit, I kind of stared at him, and went, in a pretty unprincesslike manner, 'Huh?'

'Well, everyone knows,' he said, 'that you like to write. I mean, your head is always buried in that journal. And you always get As on your papers in English. I think it's pretty obvious, Mia, that you're a writer.'

And even though I had never really thought about it before, I realized Michael was right. I mean, I am always writing in this journal. And I do compose a lot of poetry, and write a lot of notes and emails and stuff. I mean, I feel like I am *always* writing. I do it so much, I never even thought about it as being a *talent*. It's just something I do all the time, like breathing.

But now that I know what my talent is, you can bet I am going to start working on honing it. And the first thing I'm going to write is a bill to submit before the Genovian Parliament to get some rights for those sea turtles . . .

Right after I get home from going bowling with Michael and Lilly and Boris. Because even a princess has to have fun sometimes.

MEG CABOT

The
PRINCESS
DIARIES

What readers said about Meg Cabot's
The Princess Diaries 1 to 3:

"I love your books *The Princess Diaries*. I need to know how I can contact Amelia Thermopolis. I want to chat with her."

Brandi

"Mia is such an awesome character. All I want to say is keep up the good work so people like me can continue to read your books and dream of being a princess."

Maggie, 13

"You probably think I am nothing like Mia – but it's incredible how when I read the first *Princess Diaries* book, I thought it had been written about me! We're identical – apart from the whole princess thing."

Rachel, 12

"I love *The Princess Diaries* and the movie. I laughed out loud tons of times at it and annoyed my sister."

Lindsay

The PRINCESS DIARIES
Princess Club

TXT & WIN!!

Join The Princess Diaries Princess Club to get
unpublished snippets from the new Diaries &
exclusive games & competitions direct to ur mobile &
win a Princess Makeover Shopping Spree at Selfridges
in London if you give us the best reason why
U deserve the royal treatment.

To join the PDP Club and enter the competition:
Text ur date of birth and reason why U deserve
the royal treatment. Send ur message to
07950 080700

07950 080700

MEG CABOT

All American Girl

Just as a general thing, when you have saved the life of the leader of the free world, most people really want to hear about that, and, sadly, don't care to hear a long-winded description of your dog.

Sam Madison's life used to be simple – if boring.
After all, it's not much fun being the totally forgotten
middle sister between a perfect, beautiful older one
(Lucy) and a genius, precocious younger one (Rebecca).
And then there's the weird art class Sam's been made
to attend. Er, hello, what is *that* all about?

But then comes the day that changes everything – when
Sam stops a crazy psycho from assassinating the President
of the United States and becomes an instant, world-
famous, full-on celebrity. Dining at the White House sure
isn't easy for someone who only eats hamburgers and
fries, and who lives in combat boots.

In fact, there's only one compensation – David the
President's son . . .